# THE UNICORN GIRL

She was standing just inside the doorway.

I'd never seen her before, but my subconscious told me I knew this girl.

She had large, dark eyes set in an oval face Flemish masters put only on their finest angels.

Then I realized where I knew her from. In my youth I had rescued this girl from everything from evil knights to fearsome dragons in many a half-remembered dream.

## THIS WAS THE GIRL WHO TALKED TO UNICORNS

The symbol of purity and grace I had sworn to serve when I took my oath of fealty and stood vigil over my sword one long night. Ivanhoe had nothing on me when I was twelve years old. This, by Loki, was the girl of my dreams.

"Fair damsel," I heard myself saying, "How may I serve you?" She smiled, "Good sir," she said, with a voice like ripples in a silver stream, "I would that you aid me. I search for my unicorn. . . ."

# THE
# UNICORN
# GIRL

THE GREENWICH VILLAGE TRILOGY
BOOK TWO

## MICHAEL KURLAND

With a Foreword by Richard A. Lupoff

DOVER PUBLICATIONS, INC.
MINEOLA, NEW YORK

*To my unicorn girl, who will return to me.*

*Bibliographical Note*

This Dover edition, first published in 2019, is an unabridged republication of the work originally printed by Pyramid Books, New York, in 1969.

*Library of Congress Cataloging-in-Publication Data*

Names: Kurland, Michael, author. | Lupoff, Richard A., 1935– writer of foreword.
Title: The unicorn girl / Michael Kurland; with a foreword by Richard A. Lupoff.
Description: Mineola, New York: Dover Publications, Inc., 2019. | Series: The Greenwich Village trilogy; book 2 | This Dover edition, first published in 2019, is an unabridged republication of the work originally printed by Pyramid Books, New York, in 1969. | Summary: "The second book in the Greenwich Village Trilogy finds the alien-fighting hippies Mike and Chester transplanted from New York to San Francisco. When Mike meets the girl of his dreams, he and Chester join her and her circus friends on a quest in search of a lost unicorn. Psychedelic hilarity ensues as they travel through time to encounter nude Victorians, dragons, and dinosaurs"— Provided by publisher.
Identifiers: LCCN 2019022564 | ISBN 9780486838045 (trade paperback) | ISBN 0486838048 (trade paperback)
Subjects: GSAFD: Fantasy fiction. | Science fiction.
Classification: LCC PS3561.U647 U55 2019 | DDC 813/.54—dc23
LC record available at https://lccn.loc.gov/2019022564

Manufactured in the United States by LSC Communications
83804801
www.doverpublications.com

2 4 6 8 10 9 7 5 3 1

2019

# FOUR WORDS

our words: *Read. Enjoy. Trust me.*
There, I always wanted to do that. Thank you for giving me the chance. Michael Kurland's *The Unicorn Girl* is a novel about a magical world, half-mythical, half-historic, half-imaginary. Three halves? you ask. Isn't that impossible? Of course it is. That's why it's magical. It is a lost world too. A lost world called "the sixties."

What were the sixties, and when were they? First of all, they didn't start at 12:01 a.m. on January 1, 1960, nor did they end at midnight on December 31, 1969. There's a good deal of debate as to exactly when the sixties—that astonishing era that we call, as a matter of convenience, the sixties—really began. Some people argue that the era began with the election of John F. Kennedy to be president of the United States. That was November 1960. Others argue that the sixties really began with Kennedy's inauguration in January 1961 or with his assassination in November 1963. Maybe the sixties originated in England with the rise of the Beatles, Twiggy, and the Carnaby Street fashion fad, and American politics had nothing to do with it. Or them. Maybe the phenomenon (or collection of phenomena) that we call the sixties was imported to the United States.

But I know exactly when the sixties ended. They ended on that glorious day in August 1974, when Richard M. Nixon resigned the presidency of the United States. That one, I will assert with absolute conviction. I was sitting in my friend Jerry Peters's living room, when Nixon came on TV and read his statement. Jerry and I toasted the event and then I went for a walk around the neighborhood, and you could tell that an era had ended. For better or for worse, the world was made new.

The sixties were, to borrow a phrase from Chuckie Dickens, the niftiest of times and the nastiest of times. In some ways they were a flashback to the 1920s, "The Era of Wonderful Nonsense." In the twenties, sheiks wore raccoon coats and straw skimmers and slicked-down hair; shebas wore short dresses and feather boas, rolled-down stockings, and cloche hats. They all drank bathtub gin or bootleg hooch, whether they liked it or not. This was called "striking a blow for freedom," and when I was in the army thirty years later, some of our old-timers still used that expression every time they enjoyed a libation.

In the sixties, men paraded around in long hair, mustaches and beards, love beads and bell-bottom trousers. Girls (!) wore granny glasses and granny dresses and long straight shiny hair and no makeup at all, or else they opted for miniskirts and oversized sunglasses anchored to the tops of their heads and dark eye shadow and pale lipstick. For some of us, the most important questions in the world were when the Beatles were going to release their next album and whether the Jefferson Airplane's music was as trippy as the Grateful Dead's. (It wasn't.) And the drugs. Can they nab me for a series of felonies I committed years ago solely on the basis of this essay? If so, get a comfy cell warmed up 'cause here comes Arch-Criminal Number One!

I remember an icy winter's evening when my wife and I were meeting our friend Steve Stiles to celebrate his birthday. We'd bought him a baggie of something wonderful but illegal and wrapped it in bright paper and tied it with a ribbon. We'd arranged to meet in the East Village, and when Pat and I arrived, there was Steve, just across St. Mark's Place, and there was a uniformed police officer in the middle of the street, directing traffic. We certainly wouldn't jaywalk, so I hollered Steve's name, drew back my arm, and flung the gift-wrapped package skyward. It arched high over the policeman's head, through a light fall of lovely, feathery snowflakes, curved gracefully downward, and landed safely in Steve's eagerly outstretched hands. The light changed, Steve strolled across the street, passing inches from the cop, and everybody had a good laugh, never worrying about how close we'd come to three pairs of handcuffs and a ride in the paddy wagon. Instead, it was off to the Fillmore East to hear the Mothers of Invention and Sly and the Family Stone. Like our parents and grandparents in the 1920s, we, too, felt that we were "striking a blow for freedom."

Those days were long ago, and the playful lifestyle of the era seems as remote and as alien to today's world as the civilization of the druids who built Stonehenge or that of the Aztecs who constructed those mysterious pyramids in Yucatán. But if all that playfulness was the lighthearted side of the sixties, there was a serious side as well. There was the Civil Rights movement with its heroes like Dr. Martin Luther King Jr. and Rosa Parks, its villains like Bull Conner and George Wallace, and its martyrs like Chaney, Schwerner, and Goodman. There were good guys like Senator Eugene McCarthy, and bad ones like John Mitchell and Richard Daley. There was the tragedy of Kent State University and the horrifying police riot in Chicago, and behind so much of this, the Vietnam War, and behind that, the Cold War. Remember the Black Panther Party and the Youth International Party? Remember "Girls say yes to boys who say no"? Remember movies like *Easy Rider* and *Zabriskie Point*? If you don't, ask somebody who was there. We treasured the books that this new consciousness and this new spirit of questioning spawned. Ken Kesey and Hunter Thompson and Tom Robbins hit the big-time best-seller lists, and in the smaller world of science fiction there were topical novels by Michael Moorcock, Chester Anderson, Michael Kurland, Thomas Waters, Grania Davis, Norman Spinrad, and Robert Silverberg. I even wrote one myself called *Sacred Locomotive Flies*. The late Don Bensen bought it for one publisher and loved the book so much that he went to bat for it in-house. He fought so hard to get it decent treatment that he got himself fired and had to buy it all over again for another publisher, once he'd got another job.

I think of all the people I knew and loved and admired in the sixties and what became of them. The era acted like a crucible. Some of my friends and heroes were destroyed; they literally lost their lives in the flames that were those years. Others were warped, distorted, dreadfully damaged, although they managed to survive and to some degree recover. But the majority of the people I knew in that era were tempered by the heat. Like iron, they emerged as better and stronger men and women than they had been before those strange and wonderful and terrible days. And then, quite suddenly, the sixties was over. Along came the Disco Seventies and the Go-Go's Eighties and the Dot.Com Nineties, and now we are living in a new millennium unlike anything that any of us could have anticipated.

Will there ever be another era like the sixties? Oh yes, I think it's inevitable. When the proper concatenation of economic conditions, social and political circumstances, and technological advances occurs—as old H. P. Lovecraft would say, "When the stars are right"—well, we had the Roaring Twenties and the Swinging Sixties and eventually we'll have something else, something new and yet old, some fresh Era of Wonderful nonsense all over again. When? Ah, there's the rub.

But, listen, I've been getting too serious and profound for my own good or for your amusement. Michael Kurland calls *The Unicorn Girl* "an entertainment" and also "a fantasy," and he's right on both counts. We all need an entertaining fantasy now and then, and Michael has created a wonderful one for us. Just the other day I reread *The Unicorn Girl* for the first time in more than thirty years. Seamlessly, I found myself slipping from the grim present into a past that never quite existed, but nearly did, and surely should have. I found myself an invisible d'Artagnon heading off on an adventure with the three mod musketeers Anderson, Kurland, and Waters, and their lovely companions Sylvia and Dorothy. My only complaint with the adventure was that it ended too soon, but that's always a sign of a book that one loves.

Michael tells me that the memo to subscribers to *Crawdaddy* magazine is authentic, and it makes me wonder if I'll ever collect the money that *Crawdaddy* has owed me since 1969. Nah, I don't think so. The attribution to William Lindsay Gresham is also authentic. Gresham was one of the great, tragic literary talents of the twentieth century, and I commend his works to you. Other poetry in *The Unicorn Girl* is Michael's own creation and damned skillfully executed at that.

In this book, you will encounter one of the world's great natural storytellers. I've worked with Michael on several projects in recent decades and can tell you that his is one of the most startlingly creative minds I have ever encountered. We would be working along on a story or on a piece of nonfiction, and I would have thought or written myself into a seemingly inescapable literary cul-de-sac. Time after time, Michael would take over the helm and turn the narrative in a direction that I not merely hadn't thought of taking but hadn't imagined existed. And, suddenly, we were off and rolling again. That's what happens to the adventurers in *The Unicorn Girl*.

Now here's another delight you can look forward to. I mentioned that I was saddened when I'd finished reading *The Unicorn Girl*. But on this occasion, The End is not really the end at all. No! Barely had I finished reading *The Unicorn Girl* when my friend Maurice Newburn surprised me by handing me a copy of *Perchance* by Michael Kurland. What was this? I thought I knew all of Michael's books, or at least knew of them and had read most of them. But here was one I'd never even heard of. I skipped home merrily clutching the book and discovered that, twenty years after the publication of *The Unicorn Girl*, Michael had produced a—well, yes, I'll take a chance and call it a "sequel." *Perchance* is another wondrous adventure in the realm of multiple realities. Once again people go blipping from one earth-variant to another. The characters aren't the same as in *The Unicorn Girl* . . . or are they? Delbit and Exxa bear a suspicious similarity to Michael and Sylvia, and their leaps and scrapes are as breathtaking as those of their prototypes. The mood is, perhaps, a trifle darker, the tone just a little more serious, but to this reader, at least, *Perchance* reads like *The Unicorn Girl II*. *Perchance* is out of print at the moment, but if you wish hard enough, visit enough paperback dealers, cruise enough websites, you just might turn up a copy. Or, well, maybe Michael will see fit to bring *Perchance* back into print. One can certainly wish.

But for now you hold in your hands the one, the only, the original *The Unicorn Girl*. It's time to slip an old Harpers Bizarre or Strawberry Alarm Clock LP on to the turntable, pour yourself a glass of cheap wine, take off your shoes, and put up your feet. Then set fire to a little Maui wowee (if you're so inclined; don't tell anybody I encouraged you to break the law) and settle in for a trip to a wonderful half-mythical, half-historic, half-imaginary era with Michael Kurland and *The Unicorn Girl*.

*Ach*, wait a minute while I reach for my cane and hobble over to the mirror to make sure that it's really me writing this. The world has changed a hell of a lot since Michael Kurland and his chums Chester Anderson and Thomas Waters led us down those enchanted byways in the 1960s. Their magical books have for the most part been out of print for too many years, but they're back at last.

I've just read them again, and they seem quaintly innocent but irresistibly optimistic.

Those of us who have wandered out into the so-called Real World are all too often tempted to scurry back to the lands of magic and mystery. We've lost too many of our real heroes, and nowadays it seems that we're confronted by a plethora of too-real villains.

But don't give up hope, my long-ago me. The end is not yet. You'll make it from your era to mine, and together we'll make it a bit longer. We lived through both Woodstock and Altamont. Celebrate the good and survive the bad. Here. Borrow my cane, and let me lean on your shoulder, and let's march on, on into the future.

> —Richard A. Lupoff
> Castro Valley, California
> October 2019

# PROLOGUE

This is the story of how Chester Anderson and I saved the world for the second time. Chester wrote a book about the first time (*The Butterfly Kid*), so it's my turn. We both hope that it ends here, as saving the world gets to be a bit hard on the nerves.

I have been accused of writing this book to get even with Chester for his picture of me in *The Butterfly Kid*. I have also been accused of being a dinosaurian spy.

These accusations are equally true.

It was the year after the butterflies . . .

# 1

I t was a year after the butterflies. Things had sort of quieted back to normal. The reality pill, along with its audio-visual hallucinations, was a thing of the past; the supply gone, except for an odd one or two that Chester seemed to come up with whenever he felt creative. But then, when Chester felt creative, there was no telling what he'd come up with.

The only puzzle in my life at the moment was the two-week-old disappearance of a close friend and cohort of ours, Tom Waters. But then, Tom was a sometimes-professional magician, and given to disappearances. Usually he'd pop up after a few days and complain bitterly about the lack of civilization wherever he'd gone. Civilization, to Tom, was measured only by the relative abundance of peanut butter, cupcakes and cola; that being the scope of what he allowed to be food and drink.

Chester the Barefoot Anderson was on stage playing electronic harpsichord with his new group, the Elven Five. I was sitting at a table toward the back of the Trembling Womb, trying to ignore the music well enough to compose a sonnet to a lady I had recently become rather fond of. Somehow the music was making its way across well-worn synapses from the ear part of my brain to the hand part without stopping anywhere at the conscious level. When I saw that I had just written *You are lovely as a tweedle and you diddle pam my heart* as the third line, I gave up and put the notebook away.

Then I saw the girl.

She was standing just inside the doorway, not ten feet away, talking to Overly-Friendly Phil, the manager. I'd never seen her before, I was sure of that, but my subconscious told me I knew this girl. She had large, dark eyes, well set in the kind of oval face Flemish masters put only on the finest angels. Her hair was dark, color indeterminate in the coffeehouse's dim light, and folded gently about her neck and shoulders, reaching somewhere around the small of her back. She was dressed in a sort of tunic that made her boyish figure look awfully girlish. After a few seconds I realized where I knew her from. In my youth, during an extended period of reading romantic literature, I had rescued this girl from everything from evil knights to fearsome dragons in many a half-remembered dream. This was the Girl Who Talked to Unicorns: the symbol of purity and grace I had sworn to serve when I took my oath of fealty and stood vigil over my sword one long night. Ivanhoe had nothing on me when I was twelve years old. This, by Loki, was the girl of my dreams.

I couldn't help it. I got up and walked over to where they were standing. Their conversation stopped as I approached, but I, unabashed and unabashable, plunged on. I bowed low to the girl, knowing that in a few seconds I'd feel as silly as I probably looked, but living only for the moment. "Fair damsel," I heard myself saying, "how may I serve you?"

If she had giggled, I would have stalked back to my table and sulked for days. If she had giggled, none of this would have happened.

She smiled. "Good sir," she said, with a voice like ripples in a silver stream, "I would that you aid me. I search for my unicorn." She had a distinctly Cockney accent.

There were, of course, several possibilities. It might be a put-on. It could be a humorous response to my greeting. It might have deep psychological meaning, given the old unicorn legends. But somehow, I knew she was serious. This girl of my dream needed help finding her unicorn.

"Where did you lose it?" I asked.

Overly-Friendly Phil gave me a dirty look. "You know what she's talking about?" he demanded.

"Godfrey Daniel!" I explained, waving my arms and speaking above the level of the music to make myself heard. "What is there to know? The girl needs help. A damsel in distress. Surely that should be sufficient."

"Calm down," Phil said, patting me on the shoulder, a gesture I am not fond of. "Take her over to your table and talk to her. I'll send over some coffee, compliments of the house. I got enough troubles."

Taking his advice, and his free coffee, I led the unicorn girl back to my table and sat her down across from me. "Now," I said, "Tell me all about it."

The music, I noticed, had stopped. A bearded, plumpish figure was approaching the table. "Ah, Michael," the figure said in a stage murmur that carried over the intervening tables. "This Bach and Rock is hard work. *Credo.* I must rest." He sank into a chair up to his elbows, which he rested on the table. "Good evening," he said to the girl. "Are you one of Michael's, or may I scratch your back?"

"Chester," I told the girl. "Glerph. Anderson. This is."

"Glerph?" Chester asked, raising one eyebrow. He used to practice that in front of a mirror.

"And I . . . my name is Michael. Mike. Kurland." I was flustered.

"You're flustered," Chester told me. "I have a back fetish," he said to the girl, "but we'll forget it for now, since it seems to fluster Michael the Theodore Bear to hear about it."

"I am Sylvia," the girl said, looking slightly amused.

"Ah, Sylvia. From Sylvian. Creature of the wood. A delightful name. Tell me, Sylvia, what are you doing out of your enchanted wood?"

"I have lost my unicorn," she told him. "And Michael is going to help me find him." She sounded very positive.

"Glerph?" Chester asked.

"You heard the lady," I told him.

"Indeed? Ah, humph. Unicorn." Chester had often told me of his firm belief in unicorns; now he was getting a chance to prove it.

Sylvia looked at me, and then at Chester, and then back at me. "I do not understand you people. You behave very strangely. Ever since I got off the train everyone has been behaving very strangely. Perhaps it's just that I am not used to this part of the country."

"Yes," Chester assured her. "You're from Liverpool, of course." He was very proud of his ability to place different accents.

"No," Sylvia told him, "Boston."

Chester turned and glowered at the stage. I could tell he was beginning to think this was a carefully arranged practical joke. He always suspected me of practical jokes. Sometimes he was right. I, at least, never put anything in his orange juice. I was constantly finding samples of various drugs Unknown to Modern Science in mine.

Jake Holmes, the world's foremost WASP ethnic folk singer, was tuning up on the stage. I affected a strong interest in Jake's lead-in routine while Chester turned the glower on me. "Boston," Chester said.

"It's in Massachusetts Commonwealth," the girl told him.

Jake finished the tuning process and broke into song. Several teenybrats and a few of their mothers wiggled silently in their seats; their eyes intent on Jake's clean-cut, boyish profile. I wouldn't call the look one of wanton desire, but then I'm no expert on those things.

> *A very old red leather face*
> *Sits by itself watching nothing ground . . .*

"Commonwealth," Chester said clearly.

"Do you know where you misplaced your unicorn?" I asked.

"I wouldn't say that I misplaced him, exactly."

"Good for you," Chester agreed. "I wouldn't exactly say that either."

"It was when I got off the train."

"Train?" I asked,

She nodded. "The train. Adolphus seemed rather excited and nervous. We all were after what happened. Then he just bolted and ran off into the woods. It's very unlike him. The whole crew is out looking for him now."

I looked at Chester. Chester looked at me. "Do you remember when the last one was?" he asked.

I nodded. "About six years ago. They made quite a ceremony of it. The end of an era and all that sort of thing."

"The last what?" Sylvia asked. Jake sang a few more lines while Chester and I didn't answer.

> *Reality staggers and weaves*
> *Takes it away from the doorway it lives in. . . .*

"The last train," I told her. "The very last train into San Francisco before they tore up the tracks. The engine's in the Museum of Science and Industry now."

Sylvia looked puzzled. "San Francisco?"

"Or at least Oakland. The city across the bay. We're thirty miles south of it now."

"Oh," Sylvia said. "I'm afraid I know the names of few of the local towns."

I glanced at Chester. It occurred to me that I wasn't the only one capable of practical jokes.

"Is it near New Camelot?" Sylvia asked.

Chester leaned back. It was hard to tell what he was thinking. He slipped the sopranino recorder out of his belt and put it to his lips.

"At any rate, you must be mistaken about the train," Sylvia told me calmly.

"I must," I agreed, "it's a compulsion."

Jake started another song. Chester played back-of-the-room accompaniment on the recorder very softly. His face had the distinct bland look that meant he was deep in thought.

"You said the whole crew is out looking for the unicorn now?" I asked. Sylvia nodded. "What crew is that?"

"From the circus," Sylvia told me. "Everyone that wasn't too busy is out looking for Adolphus. I followed the twisty road, calling his name, until I got here. I thought he'd come to me, since I'm his keeper now and we're rather fond of each other, but he didn't. Maybe one of the others has found him by now, but I doubt it. If he won't come to me, then he won't let anyone else near him."

*Twisty road?* I wondered.

"You're from a circus?" Chester asked.

"Of course. Where else would you find a unicorn?"

"Yes," Chester agreed. "Where else indeed?" Jake had finished his set and was going offstage. In the silence Chester played a variant of an old circus song that we called "MacDougal Street Saturday Night" on the recorder. He followed that with a complicated baroque version of "Greensleeves."

"You play that well," Sylvia said.

"Thank you."

"Adolphus is quite fond of woodwind music. Do you happen to know 'Barkus Is Willing'?"

"Barkus Is Willing?"

"Yes. That's his favorite. It goes 'ta ti dum dum ti de diddly di, ta dum reedle fiddle fap.'" She had a strong, clear soprano voice.

"I, er, think I know it under a different name," Chester said. He played it for her:

"That's it," she said. "But could you play it lower?"

"Lower?" Chester asked. Putting the sopranino down, he took the alto recorder from its canvas case and started adjusting the sections in that mysterious way recorder players put their machines together. "What key?"

"*Fa,* I think."

"Right," Chester agreed. "The key of *fa* it is." He blew a note through the hardwood tube, and then a riff. "How's that?"

"Very good. Excellent," the girl agreed. "If you'd come out into the woods with me, you could play 'Barkus Is Willing' while I call Adolphus. He must be around somewhere."

I was, I freely admit, miffed. Pied Piper Anderson was doing it again. Just because he could make music come out of that petrified pipe, while the best I could ever do was a startled *pheep.*

Sylvia turned to me. She had the largest eyes I'd ever seen off of an oil painting. "Of course you'll come, Michael, and help. Please?"

Wild gryphons couldn't have kept me away.

# 2

I f you ever find yourself at a romantically lit table in the rear of an old roadhouse cum gambling casino that's been turned into an entertainment coffeehouse, staring into a beautiful girl's large eyes and telling her that she's your princess and you're going to help her find her unicorn, there's a cure. Go outside with her into the parking lot. It's impossible to keep any sort of romantic illusions intact in a parking lot—even if it fronts the Pacific Ocean thirty miles south of San Francisco. There we were, standing among orderly rows of squat electric cars and hulking gas buggies, feeling silly. At least, I was feeling silly. It was hard to tell what Chester was feeling, with his collar turned up against the damp breeze and the recorder clutched like a club in his right hand, but somehow I knew that neither of us looked like a gallant unicorn-rescuer.

Sylvia was splendid. Head erect, she marched between the rows of cars to the private sound of her own orchestra. A slightly pixilated orchestra, to judge by the skip in her step. We two followed, marching to the somber beat of a different, and much more melancholy, drummer. When we entered the glare of the single, powerful spotlight that illuminated the entrance to the driveway, Sylvia paused and looked around. For the first time the cars were lit up well enough to see clearly, and she stared at them in evident surprise. "What," she asked, pointing a delicate hand vaguely at the parked vehicles, "are these beasts?"

"You mean the cars?" I asked. Sometimes I'm a bit slow.

"Cars?"

"Automobiles," Chester explained. "Horseless carriages. Nothing a girl hunting for her unicorn would be expected to know about"

"Are they common in this part of the world?"

I looked at Chester. "Time travel?" I suggested.

"Love to," he replied. He mouthed his alto recorder and lustily blew 'Barkus Is Willing' into the night, while I tried to explain to Sylvia how it was with horseless carriages.

"Yoo, hoo, Sylvia!" a deep baritone boomed out of the dark.

"Sylvia," a mellifluous tenor added, "is that you?"

Sylvia clapped her hands together delightedly. "My friends," she exclaimed. "My comrades. Perhaps they have found Adolphus." She rose up on the toes of her tiny feet and cupped her hands to her mouth. "Here," she called. "Over here!"

There was a clopping sound, and three figures appeared in the shadows. "Sylvia," the baritone called. "We were beginning to think we'd lost you too." The figures moved toward us.

I now had a good working definition of the old phrase *too much*. This was too much. Much too much. Girls of my dreams suddenly appearing and asking me to help find their unicorns I could accept. After all, if Alice hadn't fallen down that rabbit hole, where would the world be now? But believing in Sylvia's friends would require practice. The first, in order from left to right, was a tall, slender girl with long, red hair, dressed in a Grecian style gown. I could believe in her. The second, however, was a centaur. From the waist up, he was wearing a lace-trimmed shirt, fluffy silk tie, and an eight-button jacket with wide lapels. From the waist down he was a horse. The last was a man, eight feet tall and wide as a church door, but still a man. He had the build appropriate for a giant; I could see the muscles ripple under his net shirt. When he got one step closer, I noticed something else: he had only one eye—which was centered above his broad nose.

The centaur, I could see as they came under the light, was a deep olive green. The cyclops was wearing a monocle.

"Anderson," I yelped. "You promised. You swore faithfully that you'd never do it again. How can I learn to trust you if I can't trust you?"

Chester had taken the sopranino recorder from his belt and was happily squinting at the spotlight and playing both machines at once. I refused to be impressed. He stopped playing when I prodded him and squinted at me. "What's the trouble, son?" he asked in an irritated voice.

I said calmly, "I had your solemn word that there'd be no more chemicals in my orange juice."

"Not even saltpeter," he assured me.

"I hate to doubt your word," I said . . .

"Sylvia!" the cycloptic baritone boomed.

Chester looked. His sleepy expression vanished. "Those?" he asked, prodding the air in front of him with the alto recorder.

"Those," I told him. "You see them too?"

He nodded. "What do you think we're on?"

The centaur cantered up to us. "Glad to see you're all right," he said. "Who are your friends?"

"Chester and Michael," Sylvia identified. "They're going to help us find Adolphus. This," she told us, "is Ronald."

"That's the idea," the centaur said, looking us over. "Mobilize the locals."

The cyclops and the redhead joined us and were introduced. The cyclops was named Giganto, but he assured us it was just a stage name. "My nom-de-carnival," he said. "But it's just as well, you'd never be able to pronounce my real name. It's Arcturian, of course."

*Of course? I* wondered.

The redhead was named Dorothy, and at close range she was stately and beautiful. She was beautiful at a distance too, but I'm nearsighted, and most girls look blurredly good to me at a distance. Her skin was fair, her hair was long, her features were delicate and proud, and her dress clung like the one Praxiteles sculpted on to his Aphrodite. She extended her hand to each of us in turn. I shook it, and was surprised at her strength. Chester pressed it gallantly to his lips.

"Delightful," she said. "Tell me, was't you I heard tootling upon the flageolet?"

Chester bowed, holding his alto before him like a gift offering. "Fair lady," he said, "was it pleasing to you?"

Chester always was partial to redheads.

No one, I reflected bitterly, was going to believe this tomorrow morning. Including me. I wasn't too sure that I believed it now. Then I thought of the subminiature picto I carried in my pocket in case of fire, flood or natural disaster. A color print would be reassuring to look at in the future. I slid the picto out of my pocket and checked the meter. The light multiplier was really going to have to prove itself. There was less light out here than inside the Trembling Womb. I focused as best I could on Giganto.

There was the sound of galloping; the mighty hoofbeats of the great centaur Ronald, and the picto was snatched from my hands.

"Now look," I yelled, but I was yelling at Ronald's retreating end.

"What's happening?" Giganto boomed.

Ronald swiveled around, waving the picto. "He was going to use this," he explained.

I pointed an outraged finger at the horse's front end. "What'd he do that for?"

Chester shrugged. "Bad man—black box—steal away soul," he suggested.

"Now, now," Giganto said, rolling his voice off the local mountains. "You know there's no taking pictures of the performers without a special permit. You'll get the camera back after the show."

"That's right," Dorothy agreed, shaking a stern finger at us. "It's nothing against you. It's policy."

"What show?" I asked.

"What show?" Chester echoed.

Sylvia tossed her long hair through a figure eight. "What show indeed! I'm certainly not going to take part in any show until we find Adolphus."

The bushes behind us snapped and a white figure, dimly fluorescent in the dark, appeared.

Sylvia clapped her hands. "Adolphus!"

The figure got closer and resolved itself into a man and woman clutching hands and stumbling forward together, staring with wide eyes at Ronald.

"My god!" the man declared. "That stuff was supposed to be coffee."

"I told you tamarind was some kind of dreadful drug," the woman said. Then she noticed Giganto. "Yarp!" she said, pointing. "Yarp!"

The man looked up, following her outthrust finger. "My god," he remarked, standing stock still and staring stupidly. "God, god, god."

"Now that you've reaffirmed the Trinity," Dorothy said sharply, "is there something in particular you wish?"

"No, sir," the man said. He *was* shook. "Come on, Lizzy, let's find our car." Pulling the woman behind him, he quavered off into the parking lot.

The circus people went into a huddle to discuss ways of retrieving Adolphus. And believe me, you haven't seen a huddle until you've seen one with a centaur in it I took a step closer to Chester. "Do you swear it?" I whispered.

"What?"

"No altering of my perception: No LSD, no DMT, no PJ, no reality pill, no pot, no hash . . ."

"Now you know pot couldn't do this."

"After you've had hold of it for a while, anything could do everything. I remember that meatloaf you made . . ."

"Here's what we'll do," Dorothy announced, breaking up the huddle. "We have to find Adolphus as soon as possible, preferably before morning. We'll break up into separate search parties. The two natives will go with Sylvia, since the fifing might attract him. Back down the twisty road toward camp. The rest of us will have to scatter through the woods. Have you all your silver whistles?"

Each of the circus people—cyclops—centaurs—produced a thin silver whistle and brandished it in the air. Sylvia was wearing hers on a fine silver chain around her neck. "Fine," Dorothy continued. "If you find Adolphus, or have any trouble, use the whistle."

A pair of headlights swung silently around the lot, and an electric pulled up to us. Our frightened friends were in it. The man stuck his head out and stared intently at us for a long moment. "I shall write to the *Barb* about this," he said in a tight voice.

"Don't be silly," the woman said as the car pulled away. "You know you can't write."

Giganto went off into the woods, chanting "haroom, haroom" under his breath like a rehearsing foghorn. Ronald adjusted his tie, nodded, and trotted away.

"I'd like to thank you for helping us," Dorothy said. "I'll see that you both get free passes. Good luck." She shook hands with each of us. "Watch out for Sylvia, if you would. She's very bright and capable, but she does tend to be a bit impulsive."

"I'll stay close to her," I assured Dorothy.

"Now, Dorothy, I can take care of myself. It's Adolphus we should worry about, he's never been in the wild before." Sylvia smiled up at me. "But I thank you, good sir, for your assistance."

"And your friend for his beauteous tootling," redheaded Dorothy added. "Would you consider a short gig with our circus while we're here in Nueva España?"

"Gig?" I asked.

"That's circus for job," Sylvia told me.

"I know," I said. "But somehow . . ."

"Nueva España?" Chester asked.

"Go off, people. We'll talk later." Dorothy shooed us down the narrow path leading away from the parking lot.

"Chester," I said, feeling the gravel crunch under my feet, "how long has this path been here?"

"Why," he said. Then he stopped. "Wait a second."

"What is it?" Sylvia asked, turning back to us.

"There's a stone wall all around the parking lot."

"No there isn't," Sylvia said.

"Right," I agreed. We plunged into the darkness, following the slight luminescence of the path. "Sylvia, tell me something about the circus."

"What sort of something?"

"Where the—acts—are from. Like that."

"Well . . . Adolphus is a mute, of course. Rhan Kik'hik Pyrtmyr is from Arcturus."

"Ran . . ."

"That's Giganto. That's his real name. Ronald is from somewhere in the Quagdirian Federation. He's here writing his thesis on Pre-Human Religion. Something about the emergence of the centaur myth. The circus is just a way of earning money while he's here; his grant isn't too liberal."

"I understand his problem. And the unicorn is a mute. Is that mutant?"

"Do you know of any unicorns that aren't?"

"The young lady has a point," Chester said, pausing between verses of 'Barkus Is Willing.'

"Time travel?" I again suggested.

"I don't know. Sylvia, tell me: what year is this?"

"That's silly," said Sylvia. "Nineteen thirty-six."

"I should have guessed," Chester said, regarding his recorder strangely.

"I think I hear something," Sylvia said. "Please don't play for a moment."

"Parallel time tracks," I said. "Each moving at a slightly different speed. I remember a story . . ."

"Maybe they just number the years differently," Chester suggested.

"Hush!" Sylvia whispered. "Listen to that. It certainly doesn't sound like a unicorn."

It certainly didn't. A thin, high whistling sound with undertones of bass honk, it seemed to come from all around us.

"Look," Chester said quietly.

I looked. Up in the air, slightly off to the left, hung a thing. A long, cigar-shaped thing with portholes giving off blue flashes. It was etched in the sky so sharply in red light that it gave the impression of being outlined in neon tubing. It wasn't moving.

"Look at what?" I asked Chester nonchalantly. "The flying saucer?"

Chester took a deep breath and let it out slowly. "All right," he agreed. "Look at the flying saucer. Isn't it wonderful how all you have to do is label something to understand it?"

"What is that thing?" Sylvia asked.

"It's not one of yours then," I said, "from the circus or somewhere?"

"It is not," she assured me. Her eyes were getting wide. I think this was the first time she realized there was something wrong besides a missing Adolphus.

"How far away do you think it is?" I asked Chester.

"That depends," he said. "How big is it?"

"We could triangulate," I suggested. "How's your trig?"

"Just fine," Anderson snarled. "How's yours?"

"I just thought . . ."

"At a time like this, your scientific experiments are out of place. Set up your fun-fair project tomorrow."

"I think it's important to know how far away it is," I informed Chester.

"The only thing that's important," Chester told me calmly, "is that it doesn't get any closer."

It got closer. Adding a weird *meep meep* sound to its orchestration, it started blinking an insistent red light at us and growing smoothly larger.

"Is it after us?" I asked.

"Come on," Chester said. "Let's not stay here and find out."

We started running, following the trail. Chester and I ran as fast as we could, which was pretty fast considering our sedentary lives. Sylvia loped along with us with the easy grace of a young gazelle. I decided to tell her to run faster if she could and let us catch up, but I didn't have enough breath to talk and run at the same time.

The saucer swerved slightly, correcting its aim and settling whether it was after us or not, and I tripped. Flat on my face. The gravel dug into my nose and forehead and something sharp scraped across my leg. My eyes filled with a warm, sticky wetness and I couldn't see. There was no pain and my brain seemed curiously clear. Everything was happening in slow motion. I tried to get up, but my leg wouldn't work and I fell back down. *At least,* I thought, *this will give Chester and Sylvia a better chance to get away.* I wondered whether there would someday be a brass marker at the spot where I had fallen.

Two hands tugged at my elbow, a slim arm was slid under my shoulder, and in a second I was on my feet. "Can you walk?" Sylvia inquired anxiously.

"You are the clumsiest person on the whole West Coast," panted Chester.

It is a curious trait of the human animal that in times of stress, if he doesn't panic, he tends to become overly polite and verbose. "If you two would proceed up the trail, I shall endeavor to follow as soon as possible," said I. "Not that I don't fully appreciate your stopping for me."

"Don't be silly," Chester said. "Here, wipe the blood off your face." He handed me a great square of fabric.

"Look!" Sylvia said.

"Wow!" Chester breathed.

"Where?" I asked, trying to clear my eyes. "At what? What's happening?" As soon as I could see, I looked around. There was nothing in sight but trees. "Where is it?" I yelped, turning quickly through three hundred and sixty degrees. "What happened to it?"

"It disappeared in sections," Sylvia said. "I saw it blink out."

"In sections?"

"Yars," drawled Chester in the accent he uses to explain anything he doesn't understand. "In sections, from left to right. As if it were the moon and a cloud passed in front of it."

"You don't think that could be it, do you?" I asked, staring apprehensively at the sky. "Or maybe it just turned its running lights out."

"No," Chester said. "There was something permanent about this. Besides, you can see stars through where it was. It's gone."

I brushed myself off. "I wonder what it was."

"I thought we'd already settled that," said Chester, smiling tightly at me. "It's a flying saucer."

I discovered I could walk, so we continued down the trail.

"I hope it didn't frighten Adolphus too much," Sylvia said.

I had the sudden notion that it might be what had happened to Adolphus, but I didn't say it.

"Are you all right?" Chester asked me. "Do you want to go on, or go back and get medicated?"

"I'm okay," I said. "Just a few abrasions. Continue the quest."

Sylvia took my hand and looked at me solemnly. "I'm glad, Michael the Theodore Bear, that you were not hurt." Somehow the nickname, which Chester had fastened on me when the world was young, didn't sound so silly when Sylvia said it.

"Thank you," I said.

"Then, let us find Adolphus." She sang, "Trala, tralee. Would you tootle a little, Chester?" Sylvia had amazing powers of recuperation. She skipped ahead of us on the path.

"A lot of things seem to be happening, all at once," I told Chester.

"Enemy action," he replied.

"Huh?"

"That's what you told me once. An old Army motto you had found when you were doing those war books. Once is happenstance, twice is coincidence, three times is enemy action. This is the third time."

"You have a point," I admitted as we walked down the path together. "I wonder what next?"

# BLIP

# 3

That answered my question. Something had happened, although I had no idea what. First of all, there was that *blip*. It wasn't exactly a sound, it was more like a feeling—a gut-wrenching, universe-shaking, giant *blip* of a feeling. Then there were the changes.

It was now daylight; seemingly early morning, just after dawn, but nonetheless daylight. We were still in the middle of a woods, but it was a different woods. It was more ordered: the trees seemed almost laid out in rows. The path was now a narrow brick road. A narrow—as a matter of fact—yellow brick road.

"Michael! Chester! Help!"

We ran ahead. There, sitting on yellow bricks, was Sylvia. She was crying; long, convulsive sobs that racked her thin body and left her shaking. "Help me. Please. It's awful," she gasped.

"She's hysterical," Chester said helpfully.

"What's the matter, Sylvia?" I asked, squatting down beside her. Silly question; what wasn't?

Chester bent over us. "Slap her on the back," he suggested. "Put your head between your legs," he told Sylvia.

I ignored him. "You'll be all right," I told Sylvia, taking her in my arms and holding her tightly. "Come on, now. What's the matter?"

Sylvia clutched my arm tightly for a minute and then let go and pushed me away. "Let me lie down for a while, please. That . . . thing . . . whatever it was, twisted my insides all up. Didn't you feel it?"

"We felt it," I told her, rolling my jacket up and putting it under her head, "but it didn't bother us that strongly, not physically."

"Some people get seasick and some don't," Chester added. "It's like that."

"It wasn't this bad the first time," Sylvia said, looking very pale in the bland, sunless dawn. "I'm cold."

"The first time?" Chester asked.

"Yes," she said, sitting up with my help so I could put the jacket around her instead of under her. "The first time was when the train arrived. That's when Adolphus ran away. We thought it was one of the famous Nueva España earthquakes, but it wasn't. I got sick then too; but at least the time and place stayed the same." She thought about that for a second. "Or they seemed to, they seemed to. Tell me, didn't you know about unicorns?"

"Yes," I told her. "But to us the unicorn is a mythical beast."

"And it isn't nineteen thirty-six," Chester added moodily. "That was about fifty years ago."

"I'm in the future?" Sylvia asked.

"I thought of that," I told her.

"Then we'd have unicorns," Chester explained, describing a unicorn with his hands. "And, from what you told us, interstellar travel."

"You don't travel to far planets?"

"We barely travel to near planets."

"Then . . . what is happening?"

"I'm sure we'll figure it all out," I said reassuringly. "Chester's very good at figuring things out. He has an oracle."

*Phee-ee-eep!*

"What was that?" I asked, standing up.

"It was a *pheep*," Chester informed me.

"Dorothy!" Sylvia exclaimed. "That's her signal." She tugged out her silver whistle and gave a long triple blast on it.

*Phee-ee-eeep!*

"She's coming," Sylvia said. "I wonder why none of the others answered."

"They might not have gone blip," Chester said. "They may be still wandering around in the dark looking for a unicorn. There's something to be said for that."

"Sylvia!" Dorothy called, breaking noisily through the under-brush. "Here you are. Where is everyone else?"

"Well," I said, "we're here."

"You pheeped?" Chester asked. Once he gets hold of a spelling, he seldom lets go of it.

"Pheeped?"

"Whistled," I explained.

"Oh. *Phee-ee-eep!?*"

"That's it," Chester agreed. "Pheep."

"I'm afraid we're pretty much the 'everybody else,'" I said.

"What happened, was it an earthquake?" Dorothy asked, looking around for signs of damage.

"It seems to have been more of a time quake," Chester said, and proceeded to explain what we thought we knew about what we assumed had happened.

I sat down next to Sylvia. "How are you feeling now?"

"Much better, thank you. The effects pass quickly. I'm not so cold anymore."

"That's good."

"Do you want your jacket back?"

"No, no. Keep it as long as you need it; I'm fine." People, especially girls, always assume a selfish motive if there's one available to be assumed. That's rule number five.

Dorothy pheeped a few more times, but got no answers. She put the whistle away. "I guess you're right. The silver whistle becomes merely a symbol, blown in an empty wood where none can hear."

"We're here," I reminded her.

"Left alone in a quadrilateral wood to whistle for my no-dimensional friends!" she declaimed dramatically.

"If you *want* to be left alone," I hinted.

"Leave her alone," Chester ordered. "She's merely being poetic. You, as a matter of fact (and a mind of fiction), should listen."

I spent the next few moments working that one through, putting in the necessary punctuation and sorting it out. By the time I had it, the conversation had passed me by.

"I think so, positively," Dorothy was saying.

"All right, it's settled. Let's go." Chester finished stripping the twigs and leaves off a walking stick he was manufacturing and whipped it through the air. "Onward!"

"Where are you leading us?" I demanded.

"Listen troop, yours is not to reason why . . ."

"How come every time you decide to lead you start calling me 'troop'?" I demanded. "Have you thought of what that makes the girls?"

Chester chalked the end of his walking stick and took a couple of shots on an imaginary pool table. "Never mind making the girls. Right now we go onward—out of the woods."

"Why don't we go back to the Trembling Womb?"

"Because the TW probably isn't there anymore; and that flying cigar might be."

"Onward," I agreed.

We followed the yellow brick road as it twisted through the orderly rows of trees, through hill and dale and over stream. The road went over water like a brick snake: no supports, just a single thickness of bricks humping across the stream. It managed to look like a part of nature and not an intrusion. But in this wood, nature itself was awfully ordered, with the trees planted in rows and the flowers growing in clumps and arranged with an eye to color.

"I think we're in somebody's private forest," I announced, noticing a neat line of elm running through the oak and spruce.

"More like a garden," Chester commented.

"Why garden?"

"Take a look at that patch of dahlia over there. Those reddish-purple flowers in the square plot."

"I like dahlia," Sylvia said. "They float."

The flowers filled a square about six by six feet. In front of the patch was a sign:


DAHLIA

MULTIFLORA DAHL

23:91;616   Rhumpartet Alternate


"So that's how you knew they were dahlia. I agree, it's a garden."

"Onward!"

"Ohhh . . ."

"Chester! Michael! Come look at this," yelled one of the girls, from around the next bend in the road.

We ran.

"What?" I demanded, looking around.

"That!" Sylvia pointed up.

I looked up. And up. We had entered a grove of *Sequoia Sempervirens*. Redwoods. The trees that aren't grown up until a thousand years and at least five hundred feet have passed under them.

"Look at them," Sylvia breathed. "Now I know what an oak looks like to an ant."

"This grove must be about two thousand years old," I said, looking at the girth of a nearby tree and remembering a dated slice I'd seen at a museum. "These trees were young when Julius Caesar marched against Gaul."

Chester whacked his stick against a tree, producing a satisfyingly solid *thunk*. "Now, if *these* were planted in rows, I'd worry."

We walked through the grove of giants as through a living cathedral, and our footsteps on the brick echoed among the spires and were lost.

We traveled past smaller, younger redwoods, then back to oak, and finally came to a field. It was a sort of tree kindergarten, where the saplings stood in closely-ordered rows waiting to be transplanted to their spot in the forest behind us. Across the field, some hundreds of yards away, there was a road.

"There," Chester said, pointing to where the road T'd our path. "A road. People. A town. Restaurants. Hotels. Food. Sleep. Hurray!"

I suddenly realized how tired I was, and how hungry. I stopped. "Let's rest for a minute before we go on."

Sylvia leaned against me. "Yes, let's."

"Nonsense!" Dorothy snapped. "Buck up. At least get to the road before you sit down. Here, have a lemon drop." She produced a package of lemon drops from somewhere and passed it to us.

"Right," I said, sucking on my lemon drop. "Onward and upward. Excelsior! To the road or bust." And so our tired little band traversed the field of midget trees and made it to the Great Road.

The great dirt road.

I sat down by the side of the road. "That's kind of disappointing: our main road turns out to be dirt."

*"Pace,"* Chester said, raising his walking stick in benediction. "It's still a main road, even if dirt. They do things differently in this world, or this time, or whatever."

I stretched myself out on the grass by the side of the road and prepared to make myself comfortable. "How do you mean?" I asked Chester, who was knocking around clods of dirt with his stick.

"This road's been traveled over by heavy carriages. Heavy, horse-drawn carriages. Which makes it a main road, since horse roads are seldom paved. The horses don't like it."

"How do you know all this?"

"Elementary, my dear Theodore Bear. The depth of the rut made by the wheels and their distance apart. As to their being drawn by horses . . ." Chester kicked one of the clods over to where I was resting.

"Horses," I agreed. "What makes you so smart?"

"I have my image to maintain."

"Here comes someone," Sylvia announced. She stood on tiptoe with her hands on her forehead shielding her eyes, like a James Fenimore Cooper Indian scout. If you can picture a leggy Indian scout in a minitunic, then you've got it.

Approaching us, pulled by two white horses and closely followed by a thick wave of dust, was a large, open carriage. As it got closer, we could make out the details. And the details—driver, footman and two passengers—could make us out. The carriage was white with gold trim and shaped roughly like one of Columbus's ships on large wheels. The driver and footman were perched like red and gold masts: one in front and the other in back. From inside the carriage, peering over the high sides, a male and female head regarded us. The male head was topped by a hat that looked like a golf cap six sizes too large.

The female head was wearing a yellow sunbonnet with great, stiff lace fringes.

Behind the carriage, centered in the middle of the dust cloud, rode a flatbed wagon pulled by a large, angry-looking horse and steered by a small, unhappy-looking man.

The carriage pulled to a stop in front of us. The wagon, its driver screaming a word I couldn't quite hear, jerked to a stop behind. All was quiet on the road as the golf cap looked at us and we looked at it and the dust slowly settled. Then the capped head barked a sharp "Yimmons!" and the footman jumped down and opened the carriage door. The wearer of the head stood up, revealing a slender body cased in a black suit, vest and bowtie. Taking a step forward to the door of the carriage, he pleasantly looked down his nose at us.

"Could it be that I have found here on the edge of the wood, while going on my Tuesday morning trip to town for the week's provisions—to be loaded into the wagon behind—some travelers, perchance hikers, who have misplaced their supplies and lost their way in the wood, becoming, perhaps, weary, hungry and thirsty and despairing of ever finding their way back to the company of gentlefolk (for surely, by their dress and manner they are of the gentry), after long hours, mayhap days, of their ordeal?"

He looked from one to the other of us and we stared blankly back at him.

"Well, could it be?" he barked.

"Robin, Robin," a bored female voice called from inside the coach, and the other head appeared, nodding sadly. "You're losing control."

I thought so myself.

Robin's female companion was a young woman, dressed in one of my great grandmother's dresses and carrying herself with an air that was popular when my great grandmother was a young woman. She was very handsome, in a straight-laced, old-fashioned sort of way. She, Robin and the carriage complemented each other.

Chester leaned toward me and whispered without moving his lips—one of his best tricks—"Early Victorian. *Cave.* We may have fallen into a Gothic novel."

The young man turned his nose toward his female companion. "Losing control? How so, Aunt?"

Aunt? She wasn't any older than he. Well, she didn't look any older.

She tilted her head up to what seemed to be the proper angle for conversation. "The current passion and vogue among the gentlefolk for creating and using sentences of exceeding length and complexity adds immeasurably to the pleasure of conversation when the technique is understood and properly utilized, if one can be said to utilize a vogue, and competently executed, if one can be said to execute a passion; but this is an art that should be practiced in the solitude of one's own chamber, perhaps in front of a mirror, before introducing it in public, for fear of losing one's way amidst the ebb and flow of modifiers, adjectives, adverbs, prepositions and other parts of speech within the clauses, phrases and the like that make up the sentence, and losing control of the thought that impels the word, the fact that the fancy of language can, at best, merely analog, and bubbling off into incoherence.

"In other, simpler, shorter and more direct words . . ."

Robin held up his hand to stop the flow. "No other words please, Aunt. Those will have to do. I am, as you well know, a simple country squire, and have no time for such fiddle-faddle. Well then, short and to the point. Are you travelers in need of assistance, and if so will you ride with us to the town, where such can be provided?"

"Yes and yes," I said. "And we thank you."

"Madam," Chester said to Robin's young Aunt. "In behalf of four weary travelers who appear purely by chance at this point of the road at this time, and who are sorely in need of sustenance, rest and—perhaps even more important—the humanity and friendship of those whose lands we cross, however accidentally, and upon whose bounty we must now impose, I would like to thank the both of you for stopping; surely an act of unexcelled kindness which shows the goodness of your hearts, for speaking with us; which shows your humanity, consideration and knowledge of the higher values, and, most important, for offering your aid, which must surely rank with the assistance the parable tells us was offered to that other traveler in his hour of need so long ago." He bowed stiffly from the waist.

"Oh!" said Robin's Aunt. "Well. How elegant. Robin, have our guests mount the carriage so we can get started. You sit next to me so we can talk. What did you say your name was?"

We clambered into the coach and sat ourselves on the wide, soft, leather seats. There would easily have been room for two or three more before anyone started feeling crowded. The footman took his place and the vehicle yanked to a start. When Sylvia sat down there was a moment of confusion on the part of both Robin and his aunt. They, evidently, weren't used to miniskirts. Robin seemed to be in some sort of mental crisis, staring at Sylvia's legs and then quickly away, and then back at the seat as though Sylvia had disappeared.

Aunt had herself under tight control. "Your, ah, limbs, child," she said, carefully not looking at Sylvia. "They must be cold. Here—why don't you cover them with this?" She took a sweater from the seat beside her and poked it in Sylvia's face.

"Thank you," Sylvia said, taking the sweater. "It is sort of cold." She put the sweater around her shoulders.

"I don't think you got the point," I murmured to her. "The knees, cover the knees."

"What? Why?"

"Don't ask, just do," I said, vowing to give her a complete rundown on Queen Vicky and Tony Comstock the next chance I got, since we might be here awhile. To her eternal credit, with no further questions she used the sweater as Aunt had intended.

Chester immediately launched into a sentence like a man pushing a canoe into the ocean. He was over his head in a minute, but he floundered on, drawing Robin's and Aunt's attention away from us while Sylvia made herself decent. At the last moment, when he was about to drown in parenthetical comments, he saved himself with a masterful summative clause and drove, dripping but unbowed, to a powerful and effective finish.

"Well!" Aunt repeated. "Well! Tell us about yourselves."

And he did. In rich, full-colored and patently untrue detail, Chester wove a legend of our recent past. But then we couldn't tell them the truth and expect not to be locked up. *We're from another world, or time, or something, and just arrived here on a passing blip.* Sure.

"Urgh!" went Dorothy—a sort of gargle of astonishment at the back of her throat. She was staring over the side of the carriage at something in the field beyond. I swiveled my head around and peered over the edge of the coach to see what she was looking at.

I saw.

While Chester prattled on with Robin's aunt and Robin regally surveyed his countryside, Dorothy, Sylvia and I watched as our carriage approached an orgy.

The grass was clear and green and deep, and on it six mother-naked couples frolicked in joyful abandon. Two carriages were pulled off the road onto the grass. Near them were a couple of portable tables covered with white tablecloths, on which rested wicker baskets packed with food. It was not, however, the sort of picnic that the ladies of the Church Missionary Society would have held.

The food was not yet touched. It wasn't lunchtime yet, and the picnickers were working up an appetite. Their clothes, six sets of male garb and six complete ladies' costumes, down to lace unmentionables, were neatly stacked in twelve separate piles. Their bodies, buffed bright and glistening with sweat, were arranged in six busy clusters. They ran, they jumped, they chased, they grabbed, they laughed, they were caught, and they fell down and joined together in the soft grass. It was beautiful to watch, if you went in for that sort of thing.

Sylvia licked her lips. "I don't suppose they'd ask us to join them?" I was shocked for a second until I noticed that she was staring at the baskets of food. Still, it might be a good idea to find out just what the mores of my unicorn girl's circus world were.

The scene reminded me very strongly of something out of a Victorian dirty book. The wicker baskets, the bottles of wine, the patiently-waiting horse carriages, all neatly framing the fun on the grass.

Our carriage had almost reached the scene of the action, and Chester had finally looked up from his animated conversation. He froze like a bird dog with a grouse.

"Remind you of anything?" I asked casually.

"Marin County ten years ago, but how did you know? You were in Europe."

"That's not what I meant, but never mind."

We reached the picnickers and stared over the side of the carriage at them. That is, *we* did, but our host and hostess ignored them completely and went on talking about the beauty of the autumn countryside.

Robin noticed that we were all staring at something, and looked out. "Ah, yes. The trees in autumn, the meadow, the countryside, the little changes of nature which can be seen every day as the leaves turn russet and gold and prepare to make their one trip from branch to milch; this, God's world, is where true beauty can be found and where man should seek his relaxation and find his spiritual comfort."

"Oh?" Sylvia asked innocently. "Is that what they're doing?"

The frolickers waved at us as our carriage passed them. One man, with his arms full of squirming blonde, made an obscene gesture.

I was puzzled by Robin's lack of reaction. "You," I said, gesturing at the field, "have guests, I see."

"Yes. The little creatures of the woodland make themselves at home in the fields and sport about."

I nodded and smiled, feeling very weak about the knees. Chester choked.

"What *is* the matter with you?" Aunt asked, slapping Chester heartily on the back.

Chester tried to look blasé and worldly-wise and succeeded in looking slightly bilious. "Those, ah, persons in the field," he waved an indicative arm, "out there. Very, um, interesting."

"Persons?" She leaned over and stared out of the carriage. The naked rompers, giggling and chortling, were spread out (individually as well as collectively) on the billiard-table lawn. Two by two they were forming themselves into letters and lining up to spell out a dirty word. Then, with the rapidity of long practice, they shifted to another dirty word. It's amazing the postures two human beings can assume while forming a letter; especially, I suppose, a letter in a dirty word. I resolved that, with the right partner, I'd have to try one of the letters myself. The *U* probably, I'm basically conservative.

One-half of a *T,* laughing wildly, blew a kiss at Aunt.

"What persons are these?" she asked without so much as a momentary flicker of an eyelid. "Is there somebody in our field?"

"In the field?" Robin, looking seriously concerned, peered out as a pair of melon-ripe breasts bounced by. "What would anyone be doing in our field? Where do you see them?" He stared off at the tree line. "Is someone sneaking about in our field?"

"Sneaking!" Dorothy yelped. She was suspiciously red about the ears. "The eye of man has seldom beheld such sneaking. Or of woman either!"

Aunt looked curiously at Dorothy. Chester and I looked curiously at Aunt, but she didn't notice. "Girl," she said sharply, "is something the matter? What is it? By your color, it's either dyspepsia or indecision." We had passed the picnickers and were bumping along toward the end of the field.

I looked back for one last glimpse, but the dust raised by the carriage obscured the past. It made the driver of the wagon behind us look like a World War I pilot continually coming out of a cloud bank. And hating it.

# 4

About an hour's steady bouncing later the road widened and paved itself. Around one final corner and it became the main street of a clean, dainty, well-painted town. "Well, well," Chester said, peering out at the pristine storefronts. "Disneyland."

"Welcome to West Mutton," said Robin, who was beginning to look as if he regretted his humanitarian gesture, after some brief muttering with Aunt.

Aunt took a deep, preparatory breath. "Robin and I, who make this trip to town often and are therefore well acquainted with the facilities to be found at the various hostelries and the opportunities for refreshment and amusement offered by the local establishments hereabouts, have made it our invariable custom to give our patronage to the *Sedate Duck,* which lies, as you can see, on the left side of the further street just below the Queen Mother Anne Post Office building, and would consider it an honor if you and your companions would avail yourselves of our continued hospitality and make use of the extra rooms in the suite we have permanently reserved for us in that establishment while you rest up from your ordeal and prepare to continue on your fascinating quest."

Robin glared at Aunt. "We would, we would indeed," he muttered, unconvinced.

*Quest?* I wondered. *Quest?* I should have listened more closely to Chester's story. His fictions were always committing me to a weird past and an uncertain future. It's not that Chester's unable to tell the truth, but when facts filter through his subconscious, they become woven into more pleasing patterns. As he has pointed out many times, he should not be blamed for having an artistic subconscious. I just wish it would take up painting or basket weaving, and forgo history.

I was a bit worried about our motley appearance, but the desk clerk wasn't surprised to see us. The desk clerk wouldn't have been surprised to see elephants racing teams of snails through bowls of chocolate pudding in his lobby—he worked at it. Sourly greeting our party, he bowed to Aunt, nodded to Robin and sneered at us.

Chester bristled, Sylvia sneered right back and Dorothy didn't notice. She wasn't the sort to notice a slight; she barely even saw a large.

The hotel's "boy," an undernourished sallow-faced, uniformed specimen of indeterminate age, led us up the stairs while William, the driver of the wagon that had followed us in, went off in another direction.

The suite consisted of a large, central living room, with numerous bedrooms and sitting rooms off hallways on either side. Aunt showed the girls to a room on one side and Chester and me to one on the other side. "Freshen up a bit," she commanded, "then we'll see to dinner."

I sat down on the bed nearest the window in a proprietary manner, and announced, "I could use a little dinner."

"I, personally, could have used a little lunch," Chester said. He put his coat down on the bed and glared at me as though I were somehow responsible.

"It isn't my fault," I said.

"You're my manager," Chester told me. "I expect you to manage."

"If I manage to find out what's going on, I'll be happy," I said.

"We've been blipped," Chester explained, making his "It's all so simple, Linus," gesture.

"Right," I agreed. "They're called leaves because they leave the trees in the fall. Which is why it's called fall."

"Don't worry," Chester said, rolling up his sleeves and starting to ablute in a basin on top of one of the white dressers. "You manage and I'll worry. That's known as division of labor."

"Let me give you a list of things to worry about," I suggested.

"I'll make up my own."

"If you won't discuss it, how can I be sure you're worrying about the right things? Part of my function as your manager is to make sure you worry about the right things. Otherwise I worry."

"Boy," Chester said, rubbing himself vigorously with a towel, "when you want to talk about something . . . All right, Theodore Bear, enumerate."

"Well," I held up one finger. "Where are we, why and how? Start there." I decided to take at least the outer layer of clothes off so I could get at the dirt better.

Chester beamed at me as he rebuttoned his shirt. "We're in the charming town of West—by God—Mutton. Want to wash?"

I took over the pitcher and bowl. The soap, although pleasantly scented, seemed to have a fine grit as its principal constituent "I meant in a more universal sense. Like, in what universe are we?" My shirt had plastered itself to my shoulders, using a layer of dried blood as binder. I gently peeled it off, trying not to scream too loudly when little bits of abraded skin came off with it.

"What makes you think we've changed universes? And what are you screaming about?"

"I'm screaming because it hurts; and I think we've changed universes because we're in a different universe. *Credo,* as a friend of mine would say."

"What hurts?"

"Pulling this shirt off my back," I displayed the shirt, "hurts."

"Hmm." Chester examined the shirt "Do you always bleed on your clothes?"

"Only when I'm cut," I assured him. I held up a second finger. "Two: just as an interesting side worry, something to occupy your time between big worries, how the hell do you explain whatever was going on in that field we passed?"

"Yes," the door said, opening. "How do you do that?"

"Don't you ever knock?" I asked, rebuckling my pants.

"What for?" asked Sylvia.

"Remember your tempos and mores," Dorothy suggested. They came into the room like they had a long-term lease on it and settled into the hardback chairs.

"Judging by the separation of the bedrooms by sex," I said, "I'm surprised they let you in here."

"We snuck," Sylvia said, with a touch of giggle in her voice.

Dorothy informed us: "I am not in the habit of letting someone else decide what I can and cannot do. I wished to consult with you to decide what our next actions should be, and so I did."

"You didn't march across the living room," Sylvia said. "You snuck, like me."

"Well," Dorothy said. "That Aunt person seemed to be making such a point of segregating us by sex, I preferred not to antagonize her unnecessarily.

"Do either of you two gentlemen have any idea of what's going on around here?" Sylvia asked.

"Here?" Chester sounded.

"You know. I mean all over—all around us. The ship and the woods and the blap and Ronnie disappearing and the circus disappearing and these people—Robin and his aunt—and this town and those people in the field and . . . and : . ." Sylvia bit her lip and held her breath to try to stop from crying, but it wasn't working. A small sob escaped from between her clenched teeth.

"Now," I said, wrapping my arms around her and gathering her to me. "It isn't that bad, honest It just *seems* that bad."

Dorothy looked at us scornfully. She couldn't figure out what all the fuss was about.

"It is a problem," Chester confessed. He pulled a small notebook out of his back pocket. "I've taken a few notes," he said, flipping through the book. "Let's see; the first chapter of my new novel, *And Then I Told God;* charts on my correlation of the *Talmud* and the *I Ching;* the addresses of forty-five cemeteries in the Los Angeles area; the phone number of the archives room at the Boston Public Library. . . ."

"When did you take these notes?" I asked. "I don't remember you taking notes."

Chester looked indignant "I *always* take notes. You know what a bad memory I have. Now then: twenty-seven common substances that will give you a high; notes for a review of Lennon's *Prelude in B Flat Until the Neighbors Complain;* six exotic ways to use canned peaches. . . ."

"A recipe?" I asked in surprise.

Chester merely looked up. "No. Where was I? Why can't I ever find anything in this book?"

"You should write things in order instead of skipping around the pages," I suggested.

"Then I could only find things by remembering the order I wrote them. I find random access more useful. That way I have to go over everything I wrote every time I use the book. It's a form of cross-fertilization. Hmm: a phone number with no name attached, which is annoying; a name with no memory attached—exasperating; a map of the battle of Jeppet . . . Hrmph! One of your love poems; what's that doing in my notebook? Well: a list of the strategic places to plant firebombs in Austin, Texas. The names of four ducks. Ah! Here we are."

"Four ducks?" Dorothy asked, fascinated by the list.

"Mallard is the only duck name I can think of offhand," I volunteered.

"Not that sort of names," Chester snorted, flipping back to the page and showing it to me. I read aloud:

HUEY, DEWEY, DONALD, DAISY.

"The names of four ducks," I admitted, "What are they doing in your notebook?"

"I don't remember, but if you'd like me to make up a story . . ."

"No thanks," I said. "Let's hear your notes."

"Fine. My notes. There are six things I have written down here."

We all leaned forward and adjusted ourselves, ready to hear the word. Somehow, when you write something down, it becomes more important. The value squares when it's typed, and cubes when it's put into print. Chester explained this carefully to me when he talked me into buying an old web press with him. Now that most people don't read, the value of the printed word has increased even more, because it has become mysterious.

"Thing one," Chester read. "It's probable that the UFO we saw has something to do with the blip we felt."

"UFO?" Sylvia asked.

"Unidentified," I explained, "flying object."

"Oh," Sylvia said. "So that's what it was."

Chester said, "Name magic. Now she knows. Ha!"

"What does he mean?" Sylvia asked.

"Nothing at all," I told her. "Chester isn't happy unless he's obscurely insulting or insultingly obscure at least three times a day."

"Oh," Sylvia said. She smiled sweetly at Chester. "I'm glad to be able to keep you happy."

"Let us eschew dissension," Dorothy said, eying Chester, who was hefting the notebook like a baseball. "Go on."

"Thing two," Chester said, returning to his notes. "We have been on—we are on—a journey together; not through time or space, but between time and space."

"How's that again?" I asked.

"Parallel time tracks," Chester explained.

"That's What I said before," I told him.

He ignored me. "Thing three: there's something wrong with the system."

"What system?" Dorothy asked.

"Look," Chester said, "you and I, you," he waved a collective hand, "and us; we're from different time tracks, you agree?"

"If that's what it is," Dorothy nodded. "We're from different something. The unicorn a mythical beast indeed!"

"And you've been through two blips—transfers—one of which we shared with you."

"Horrible, nasty things," Sylvia said with a shudder.

"Well, that's it. Proof."

"How is that proof?" I asked.

Dorothy demanded, "Proof of what?"

Chester looked pained at our ignorance. "Proof that there's something seriously wrong with the system, that the orchestra's got a sour bassoon. Look, have you ever heard of anything like this before? Ever?"

"No," Dorothy admitted.

"Well, what *that* means is that it doesn't happen very often. Now it's happened to one small group of people—us—twice in a short time. That would seem to indicate that," he ticked a finger, "something's seriously out of whack in general, or," he ticked the next finger, "someone's out to get us in particular; which I feel is quite unlikely. At times in my paranoid past I would have assumed that the Universe is teaming up to get me, but now I'm more objective and I don't believe that. I *think* it, but I don't believe it."

"You keep cheerful notes," Sylvia said. "What's next?"

"Thing four," Chester continued, peering closely at his notes. "Hmm. I must have written this from the moving carriage, it's hard to read."

"Your ant-tracks are always hard to read," I told him. "What do you think it says?"

"It looks like 'the durgs are black and have legs,' but I have no idea what that means."

"Let's do our best not to run into any durgs," I suggested. "Just in case your notebook has developed a propensity for prognostication."

"I shall say no sooth," Chester assured me. "I read on. Thing five seems sort of obvious, but sometimes it's the obvious that needs saying. So: this time-space we're in is occupied mostly by Victorians. Real, stuffy, up-tight Victorians. And those people we passed in the field, who were obviously something else."

"And us," Dorothy added.

"Right."

"Those, er, people in the field," I said, using Chester's circumlocution, "what about them? They're not exactly Victorian. Besides, Robin and his aunt didn't even seem to notice them."

"There are none so blind," Chester said sagely, "as those with no eyes."

"I'll grant you that," I agreed.

"What does he mean?" Sylvia asked.

"Who knows?" I explained. "But don't argue with him, he gets nasty."

Chester ignored me. "That brings me to my last point. Thing six: we must seek more information, because we really have no idea what's going on."

"Oh, that's what he means."

"Now it's all clear to me," Dorothy said.

"When you figure out what's going on," I suggested, "let me know."

"Don't be sarcastic," Chester said. "I didn't say I had all the answers. I was just trying to state some of the questions. Questions first, then answers; it's one of the oldest rules."

Dinner was quite an occasion. We were supplied by the hotel staff, at the instigation of Robin's aunt no doubt, with fresh costumes. I say costumes advisedly. Mine gave me the general appearance of Nigel Bruce playing Dr. Watson. Chester's turned him into an unjovial Pickwick. All through dinner he had an unhappy, constrained look. His cravat had been fastened too tight, and he didn't know how to loosen it without taking it off.

The dinner was held in a private dining room downstairs. There were nine guests, who I suspect were invited to take a look at us. We were introduced to them as they came in: Mr. Falkenburg, Colonel Montmorency, Dame Wycouth, Colonel and Mrs. Blake, Lady Caren Shashlic, Professor M. Nant, Lord Goldberg and Mr. Hame Seulhomme, Esquire.

Aunt introduced us as distressed travelers, who had a fascinating tale of adventure to tell.

Colonel Blake stood up. A slender man, immaculately dressed in a dark, pin-stripe, double-breasted suit, with a darker vest and a black, flowing tie; he carried himself with an ineffable air of complete authority that was enhanced by his neatly-trimmed, spade, salt and pepper beard and his miter-top brushcut. The only anomaly in his appearance was the fleeting glimpse we had when he stood up of bright-red socks. The group turned to him as a congregation turns to its rabbi, and waited for the word. It came.

"We welcome you to our community, fellow travelers on the Road of Life, in the name of the town leaders," he nodded to those around him and flicked an imaginary dust mote off his sleeve, "in the name of common intelligentsia, for I can see that you are of us, in the name of biblical commerce; as that merchant of old was aided in his hour of need, in the name of human decency, in the name of progress, in the name of trust and kindness, in the name of unity, in the interest of your safety and our own well-being, in the dining room at this time, in the interlude between meeting and eating," here he paused for a laugh, which he didn't get, "in the, ah, hope that you will favor us with an account of your adventures, both to sympathize with you for having suffered the ordeal while empathizing with the heroic adventure and to learn thereby what we must prepare for in this rapidly changing world, which seems to be doing so much by itself these days, without waiting for our guidance, in recognition of the mutual good we can do each other (and fully aware of the redundancy implicit in the phrase 'mutual good'), allow me to take this time to speak for all of us here and welcome you, ladies and gentlemen, to our town, to our hospitality and to this dinner."

All this, you understand, was done with one breath. The assemblage broke into polite applause, and Colonel Blake nodded stiffly several times, like a satisfied puppet.

"On behalf of our unfortunate little group," Chester puffed, "I thank you, singly and collectively, for your hospitality and assistance." Everyone beamed at the politeness, although they would probably have been more pleased if the sentence were a couple of yards longer. But the servants were starting to put the food on the table, and the odor wafted to our hunger-sensitized noses and precluded long sentences. The only interest we had was in cutting the preliminaries short and getting to the food. After that, a good night's sleep would be in order; but first the food.

Two by two the guests made their way to the table. Colonel and Mrs. Blake led the way, the Colonel beaming and pompous, his lady gleaming and dainty. The gleaming came from two square yards of assorted gems that had been strung together and laid out to dry across her ample breastworks. The next pair were Robin and his aunt. Auntie had also bedecked herself with a considerable amount of mineral finery. Dame Wycouth, supported by Mister Falkenburg, swept by next in line to the festive board.

"All this couldn't be just for us," I whispered to Chester.

"Of course not," Chester agreed. "A gathering like this couldn't have been arranged on such short notice, so it must have been prearranged. I have experimentally verified this hypothesis."

"How?"

"By asking. Robin's aunt confirms that this affair was planned over two weeks ago, and the only change was the hasty approval of us as special guests."

"I really should have listened to the story you told her," I commented. "It must have been good."

"It was," Chester assured me. We made our way to the table.

The food was excellent, the service was superb and the conversation was scintillating. I got the impression that we were being held, conversationally, for the last course. The guests spoke freely, and even eagerly to us, but they reserved questions about us or our experiences until the end of the meal. The talk at the table was unique in one respect: only one person spoke at a time. Robin's aunt served as a sort of moderator, while people around the table threw questions and comments at each other. The object of the game seemed to be to answer in only one sentence, of whatever length was required. Accuracy, and even sense, gave way to form. The principal trouble was that, as the sentence got longer and more unwieldy the speaker would forget exactly what modifier, verb, or even noun he had used at the start of the ponderous construction and proceed off in lateral branches of thought that would have little bearing on the concept that he, despite the appeal of glittering phrase or the easy lengthening effect of the added unimportant, but fine-sounding clause would have little . . .

It takes practice.

Chester held his own quite well during the verbal riposte. I managed to usually have my mouth full just when I was asked something, so one of my three companions would come to my rescue after I had spluttered "Arb grubble hooh asgud me sulch," and finish for me. Which was probably just as well. The girls smiled a lot and, following Chester's instructions, answered all questions with earnest vagueness. Pretty girls have a corner on the earnest vagueness market.

The heavy table creaked under the weight of the salvers of succulent roast beasts and the platters piled with engravied legumes trucked in by the hoards of servile servitors who serviced each of the assemblage. I won't tell you whose notebook I copied that line from. Anyway, the image is right. There we were, stuffing ourselves while this bunch of skinny servants leaped around waiting on us. It was impossible to empty a plate without having another thrust in front of you. No sooner could you finish one glass of chilled, white wine, savoring its hearty, if naive tartness, than a delicate, grapey rosé, presumptuous and a bit early, but worthy of the palate, would be plopped in its place. The dialogue I got from Colonel Blake, who connoisseured himself greatly, loudly and often.

About halfway through the burnt mooseliver course I picked up my crystal water goblet and, holding it in the Colonel's characteristic three-fingered grip, waved it in exaggerated horizontal circles in front of me. "Hem!" I said. "Ahem. Hem. Humph."

Chester saw what I was doing and gave me warning glance 36(a), subtitled "This is neither the time nor the place and I'll get you later," but I was too far gone to stop. The scent of the kill was in my nostrils. Sylvia, next to me, was watching, unsure of what was happening; and by that empathy which unites people with a common bond, Dorothy at the far end of the table was staring at me, sure something was going on. It took a while before I had attracted the attention of our hosts, but I waited.

Finally the Colonel himself noticed me, and I went on to Phase Two. "Hem. Hem. Harrumph, a-hem, a-hem, ahem, hoom, hoom." Perhaps a bit clearer than the Colonel, but no louder. His very words. "Ahemph! Ah!" I bounced the goblet once or twice to cause ripples to flow across the surface of the water, but not enough to spill a drop. Puckering my lips like a man about to kiss a camel, I brought my mouth down to the glass, tilted it and allowed a few drops of water to run between my camel-kissing lips.

I thrust the glass away from me, holding it in midair, and with the pinky of my other hand traced small objects in the air above my head. I swished the liquid back and forth, meditatively, between my teeth; making a gurgling sound. I could tell I had their interest. Noisily, I swallowed.

I smacked my lips, head back in a reflective manner, and tasted the air. Slowly, ever so slowly, I put down the glass and closed my eyes. "Ah, yes," I said. "Yes, yes, yes. Water."

There was a choked-off giggle to my left, and I very carefully avoided looking at Sylvia.

"Water. The very water. Fine water. Cool water, but not artificially cooled. Spring water, I would say. Yes, spring water. Definitely. Naive, unpretentious spring water. A bit presumptuous, perhaps; but that, after all, is the prerogative of a truly great water." I raised the goblet for another taste, smacking my lips. "Yes, the second taste, or *le deuxième* as we connoisseurs call it, confirms my first thought, or *le premier*. Spring water. *Western* spring water. Just a trace, perhaps, of melting snow from mountain brooks that feed the spring. Also traces of sulfur, antimony, calcium, lead (probably from the pipes), iron, or its oxide, zinc, various ammonias and phosphates and a hint, just a hint of iodine. Also," I wrinkled my nose slightly, "I would say that there have been fish in this water."

I opened my eyes and looked about. A monumental silence hung over the table, and everyone avoided my eye. Everyone except the Colonel. "Come now," he said. "No iodine, surely."

"Oh?" I said. "I would have thought—just the slightest bit. But perhaps not." The man was impervious. There are none so humorless as those who will not see themselves.

"Have you," Aunt asked Chester, "read the Reverend Dodgson's *Alice's Adventures Under the Ground?* A rather profound work, I thought." This successfully changed the subject.

Along with Chester's exposition on how to best mock a turtle, came dessert. Cakes, pies and puddings, each carried around the table by a dessert waitress. Each course, it seemed, had its own slaves. The maître de dessert stood by the door, overseeing his girls' handling of the dessert-filled trays. He looked familiar.

"Have you ever seen that man before?" I asked Sylvia.

"Which man?"

"The one by the door in the monkey suit."

"No, I don't think so."

"Ignore the clothes and wait till he smiles."

Sylvia studied the man for a moment. "Yes! That grin—it's the man from the field. The one who followed behind the carriage laughing at us. I didn't recognize him with his clothes on."

"You are," I told her, "a spirit of no common rate."

"What do you think he's doing here?"

"I imagine he's in the employ of the kitchen."

"Well, he has interesting hobbies."

The dinner guests dug into their varied desserts, and there was a pause in the conversation while they paced their pastries. I tried to figure out how to make room in my overstretched stomach for hot apple tart.

The serving girls backed off and looked at their boss. He nodded. In unison, like the chorus line at Minsky's, they unhooked the blousefronts of their prim costumes, shrugged and wriggled free of the fabric, and stepped forward and out of the fallen garments. They were wearing nothing else.

Sylvia, eyes round, nudged me with her elbow.

"I see," I said.

She whispered, "Yes, but nobody else seems to."

"You're right." Looking around the table, the only others who seemed aware of the nude show were Chester, who was nonchalantly eating his raisin pudding while watching, and Dorothy, who was just watching. Chester looked at me and slowly nodded his head back and forth. Everyone else at the table was calmly eating, apparently completely unaware of their naked serving wenches. I decided that Chester was right. If our hosts didn't see what was happening, it wouldn't be wise for us to.

The three bare beauties approached the table. Each of them stationed herself behind one of the ladies and, slowly and gently, started removing necklaces and bracelets. They carefully unpinned Aunt's tiara and took it with her earrings. Aunt went on talking and eating as though nothing unusual was happening.

After they had cleaned all that glitters from the ladies, sparing only Sylvia and Dorothy, whose only glitter at the moment was internal, the three nymphs kissed each of the men on the cheek in a gesture of either fair play or contempt, and departed, skipping, through the kitchen door.

"Well," Aunt said, stretching daintily, "shall we allow the men to retire to their cigars and brandy?"

"That's good of you, Madam. If you ladies would excuse us?" The Colonel rose and bowed politely, which was quite an ability, considering what he'd eaten. If I'd leaned that far forward, I would have fallen on my face. We men followed him into the next room in our stately, stuffed way to indulge in a little mantalk.

There's nothing that makes a man feel so much like a man as to get off in a corner and tell suggestive stories. The stories these men were telling suggested only lack of experience and limited imaginations.

Chester and I left after about ten minutes of this, pleading extreme tiredness—which was no exaggeration. I may have stayed awake for a whole forty seconds after my head hit the pillow.

The next morning I woke up with the sun glaring through the window right into my eyes. I had no idea how long the sun had been there, but I just wanted it to go away. I covered my head and rolled over.

"Michael," Chester bleated, "I'm glad to see that you're finally awake."

"I wouldn't exactly call it awake," I groaned.

"It'll have to do. We have some serious business to discuss, quickly."

"Later," I suggested, putting the pillow over my head. "Come back later, and we'll talk."

"You don't think I enjoy trying to wake you up, do you?"

"I'm not really interested in your perversions. Let me alone."

"Tomorrow, I promise."

"Have you got any coffee?" I asked, peering out from under the pillow.

"Certainly."

"Good. Drink a cup. Drink two cups. Go away!"

"When important decisions are to be made," Chester said, "Michael the Theodore Bear will be the first to sleep through them."

"I can outsleep you," I informed Chester, "in my think."

"My point exactly." Chester sulked by the window. "Now, now, look at that!" he said, sticking his head out and staring.

"You won't catch me with that one," I told him. "But, as long as I'm awake anyhow, with all this talking, I might as well get up and see what you're looking at." I rolled out of bed, got up and went to the window. There on the street, two stories below, stalked a strange assortment of people. Two Spanish conquistadores, muskets at ready, took the lead. Behind them, strung out in what my sergeant had called eskirmisher formation, were three Roman legionnaires in winter dress, an angry-looking Norseman and a Pennsylvania state trooper. The group slowly passed out of sight toward the center of town.

"What," I asked Chester, "was that?"

"Why are you whispering?"

"I always speak quietly in the face of the unknown," I told him. "Don't try to change the subject."

"We should have you face the unknown more often. I don't know how that group got together, but it shows that we aren't the only ones suffering from confusion of time lines."

"Confusion is the right word. Where's that coffee?"

"There's a pitcher on the dresser all creamed and sugared, help yourself."

"You know I don't take sugar," I complained.

"Next to the pitcher you will find a pair of tweezers, with which you may, if you choose, occupy yourself by removing the sugar, grain by grain, from the coffee."

"Urph," I said, pouring a mug of coffee. "Thanks." I drank the coffee, which had a metallic taste, poured myself a second cup and started struggling into my clothes. "The fog is lifting. By the end of cup two I'll be awake enough to talk."

"See," Chester said. "Dependence on drugs is an insidious thing." He came away from the window. "Well, that group down there shows why our hosts required so little explanation from us. They've seen others."

"That's why they're so friendly," I offered. "They've captured us for dissection." I inspected my face critically in the mirror. "I need a shave."

"Go ahead," Chester instructed, indicating the implements neatly displayed on the towel next to the washbowl. "Help yourself, I'm done."

I picked up the straight razor and examined it. "I've never used one of these. I'll probably slit my throat."

"That will be a good start on the dissection. When you've bled to death, I'll finish shaving you so you make a handsome corpse."

"Thanks." I stropped the razor against the leather block.

"Well," Chester said, watching with a critical eye as I scraped my throat.

"Well what?"

"What's our plan? What do we do from here?"

"How," I demanded, "should I know?"

"You're the manager."

"You're awake. You've had time to think—or whatever. You tell me."

"Well, I've been thinking."

"Good."

"I've made some notes." Chester pulled out his little notebook.

"I've been here before," I told him.

"Have you ever stopped to consider," Chester asked me, "how interesting you'd look if you cut off your right ear?"

I carefully put the razor down and wiped off my face. "Okay, let's hear it. Read the notes."

"It's about that scene last night. You remember what happened last night?"

"I presume you mean the Great Naked Jewel Theft."

"Yes. Did you notice anything about that?"

"Three female bodies. I noticed them in great detail."

"Something beyond the physical details—don't snicker like that—something indicative of the nature of the problem."

"?"

Chester flipped through his notebook. "Here. It's a question of taboo. These people are primitively Victorian. There are taboos on certain types of activity—sex, certainly, and probably several others. What is taboo cannot be gone into. It cannot be done, it cannot be thought about, it cannot be allowed to exist, it cannot be seen. Therefore it is *not* seen, even when it happens."

"You mean those people didn't see what was going on?"

"That's my thought."

"But nudeness—or is it nakedity—isn't sex. Not all by itself."

"To you, no; to them, yes."

"Then how do they, er, propagate?"

"In the dark, milad, in the dark."

"Wow. Say, how are they going to explain the disappearance of all those jewels?"

"Sneak thieves in the night, I guess." Chester looked smug and self-satisfied. But he had found the answer. To you, reading this, it probably was no problem from the start; you had it figured out. But imagine actually being there. If you see a group of people behaving in a peculiar manner and another group ignoring it, do you assume that group *B* is unable to see group *A* or just that they don't care? When there's a mugging and forty people walk by without doing anything, is it because they don't see what's happening?

"It furthers one," Chester told me, "to have a plan. I have rolled the coins and the oracle has so said."

"I didn't know you had a pocket *I Ching*."

"I've committed the work to memory. The Baynes rendering of the Wilhelm translation, of course. Also my addendum. It furthers one to cross the Grand Concourse. It furthers one to have somewhere to go."

"Where?"

"In the times of trouble, the wise man listens carefully to his advisors. One may use two bowls for the offering." Chester tapped his chest. "I am the wise man." He pointed a digit at me. "You are my advisors."

"All of them?"

"You are a man of many parts."

"No more than the usual number."

"Come on," Chester commanded. "The *Ching* said I should listen to my advisors. Give."

"Did the *I Ching* say what I should do?"

"It furthers one to play one's proper role. It furthers one to seek one's place. It furthers you to make like a manager."

"The *I Ching* said that?"

"Ask it yourself."

"And trust to *your* memory and honesty for an answer?"

Chester looked insulted. "There are some things that are below me."

"Yes, I've seen some of them. Wait a second." I carefully took out my wallet and opened the little compartment that held my three coins. They were silver dimes—real silver, dating back to 1958, 1962 and 1964. My good luck pieces, not that I believe in luck. "Stand back." I kneeled on the carpet in the ancient, prayerful attitude of the crap shooter, shook the coins between my fingers and cast them out. Two heads and a tail.

Chester had his little notebook out, turned to the back section where he kept permanent record of what either of us has asked the *Ching,* and the answers. I call it *The Wit and Wisdom of an Ancient Chinese Sage,* or *Backtalk from a Book.* "Eight," he said, writing down the first line. "The young yin. Firm, female and at rest. Proceed."

I cast again. Two tails and a head.

"Seven. The young yang. Unmoving male." He placed the second line above the first. "And again."

*"Faites vos coupes, messieurs et mesdames,"* I intoned. "Are all bets down?"

I cast the dimes again and they skittered across the rug. One of them couldn't make up its mind for a moment, and then it flopped over with the others. Chester notated. "Another seven, and the bottom trigram is complete, with no (count them, no) moving lines. It's the trigram *Sun,* the Gentle, which is Wind." Chester contemplated what he had drawn for a moment with that wide grin which appears when he is deep in thought and shouldn't be disturbed. The next step is a wide grin combined with an intent look. This means he is deep inside his own head, and cannot be disturbed, or even located.

For those who have so far managed to steer clear of ancient Chinese oracles, the trigram *Sun* looks like this:

---
---
---　　---

Remember that it is constructed from the bottom up, like a house.

"There are many possibilities," said Chester. "Continue." I threw the coins again, and got three heads. "Aha! A nine, and therefore the old yang. A moving line. A change from the *Book of Changes."* Chester looked as pleased as if the coins had done it on purpose, just for him. Perhaps they had at that. The only thing I can tell you is that sometimes I get the curious feeling that a group of Chinese sages who died before Confucius was born, and who never dreamed of a language called English, are talking to me from the other side of this English version of a German translation of a Chinese text. The moving line was one that changes from yang to yin, giving us a specific reading on that line (number four, counting up) and changing the trigram to give us a second hexagram to consider. Thus, you see, the *Book of Changes*.

I tossed again, for another nine, a second changing line. Then the sixth, and final, time; a seven: yang, solid, unchanging. The second trigram was complete:

```
————————
————————
————————
```

With changes in lines four and five, to create:

```
————————
——  ——
——  ——
```

This gave us the primary hexagram:

```
————————              ————————
————————              ——  ——
————————              ——  ——
———————— which changed to: ————————
————————              ————————
——  ——                ——  ——  I hope that's clear.
```

"The trigram is *Ch'ien,* The Creative, or Heaven. A good one. It changes to Keeping Still, *Kën,* which is described as being like an inverted bowl." Chester consulted the back page of his notebook. "Ah, so I thought. *Ch'ien* on top of *Sun* gives us hexagram forty-four: *Kou:* Coming to Meet. The image is that of wind under heaven. Which, if I remember correctly, is described as how a prince acts when disseminating his commands and proclaiming them to the four quarters of heaven."

"You remember correctly," I told him. "I can tell by the look on your face. What's the rest?"

"I don't remember. I thought I was pretty good to get that much."

"I'm proud of you," I told him. "But that will teach me not to consult an oracle I don't have with me. It's like trying to make a long-distance call by yelling into a rock."

"A rock?"

"A roll?"

"Damn!" Chester suddenly sat down. Since there was no chair under him, he ended up on the floor, but didn't seem to notice.

"It wasn't that bad," I insisted.

"I've been using the *Ching* all morning to clarify our position," he said, slapping at his pockets like he smelled smoke, "and getting annoyed because I couldn't remember enough of the text to get the full meaning in several of the readings."

"That would be annoying," I admitted.

"I have one with me," Chester said, "and I forgot."

"One what?"

Chester took his jacket off and dug deep into his right-hand pocket, past the ripped-out bottom and toward the back of the jacket lining. He pulled out his hand with a grandiloquent gesture, a long, silver tube clutched in his fist "This!"

"So that's what happened to my pocket telescope," I said.

"Your pocket telescope went back to Captain Video with the decoder ring," Chester said, squinting at his toy. "This is a microfax reader, complete with about thirty books. Including . . ."

"Let me guess," I said. "Not, by any chance, the collected works of Chester V. J. Anderson?"

"That, too," he admitted. "You'll have to try it. It's so much easier than lugging around that briefcase you always manage to accidentally have with you."

"That's unfair," I said. "I used to carry around a copy of your book of poems until you borrowed it from me."

"I remember," Chester said. "You used to read it to every girl you were trying to take to bed. I don't think it's right to use my poetry to make your girls."

"Why not?" I asked. "Considering some of the things you've used . . ."

"Wharf!"

"I was just kidding."

"This thing's stuck—it won't go on. Could the batteries be dead?"

"They haven't invented electricity yet in this world. You know that nothing exists until after it's been invented."

"Make this work," Chester said, handing the tube to me. I looked it over for a minute and then unscrewed the back section where the battery and bulb were, exposing the focusing lens.

"Hold it up to the light."

Chester took it back. "It's very dull," he complained, "and the wrong book's in the viewing field." He twiddled with the selector ring. "Ah, the action's mechanical. Here we are now: Philosophy and Divination, Ancient Chinese, for the use of. A little fine tuning, and we arrive at forty-two, forty-three, forty-four! Coming to Meet. Hrmph. The judgment. Of course, how could I forget?"

"What does it say?"

"'The maiden is powerful. One should not marry such a maiden.' It speaks of a bold girl who lightly surrenders herself, and thus seizes power."

"Or perhaps necklaces," I suggested.

"Nine in the fourth place," Chester continued, reading the comment on the first moving line. "No fish in the tank. This leads to misfortune."

"Huh?"

"Nine in the fifth place: 'A melon covered with willow leaves. Hidden lines. Then it drops down to one from heaven.'"

"This is no time," I complained to a nameless Ancient Chinese Sage, "to be vague."

"That brings us," Chester said, "to the hexagram created by the changes: number eighteen, *Ku*, or Decay." He twisted the control ring.

"Decay. Swell. Cheerful book you've got there. What does it mean?"

"It's *your* reading," Chester pointed out.

I glared at him. In my best singsong voice, I intoned:

*I do not love thee, C. V. J.*
*Why this should be I cannot say.*
*But this I'll tell thee every day,*
*I do not love thee, C. V. J.*

"I'll control my grief," Chester said. "Here we are: 'Work on what has been spoiled has supreme success. It furthers one to cross the great water. Before the starting point, three days. After the starting point, three days.'"

"That's it?" I asked.

Chester shrugged. "There's a lot more. Try this: 'Thus the superior man stirs up people. . . .' What was that?"

It sounded like the people were stirring up. From somewhere outside our door was coming the sound of milling people, slamming doors, stamping feet and angry voices. "I don't know," I said. "Did you order breakfast sent up?"

"I lack your vast experience with hotels," Chester said, slipping his jacket on and walking gingerly to the door, "but that doesn't sound like room service to me."

"You may be right," I admitted. I finished dressing and joined him at the door. "Take a look. Anything in sight?"

Chester peeked around the door. "No. They must be in the main room."

"Let's go see," I suggested.

"I don't like the sound of it," Chester said. "Maybe we should stay here."

"If they're after us we're at a dead end here. Outside we have more room to maneuver."

"I suppose so," Chester said, stepping aside. "Go ahead, I'll be right behind you."

"Someday I'll have to get a working definition of 'manager' from you," I said. I went out into the hall and started tiptoeing toward the closed door to the main room.

"All of my definitions work," Chester said, taking up the rear.

"Close the door," I whispered. The noise got louder as we approached, and we could make out individual voices.

| | |
|---|---|
| VOICE 1: | They did it. Of course they did. They must have done it. Who says they didn't? |
| VOICE 2: | We really should give them the benefit of a doubt. Hold them for trial. *Then* hang them. It's only right. |
| VOICE 3: | Suppose they didn't do it? |
| VOICE 1: | You saying they didn't do it? You in it with them? |
| VOICE 3: | I guess you're right. They must have done it. |
| VOICE 4: | Come on, you two, what'd you do with the jewelry? You may as well tell us. We'll get your boyfriends out here as soon as the marshal arrives. |
| VOICE 1: | Why wait for the marshal? Let's string 'em up now! |
| VOICE 2: | Dirty sneak thieves. Give them a meal and a place to sleep, and this is how they pay you back. Sneak thieves. In the night, when a man's sleeping. Taking your goods. It's a crime. [I think this was Robin.] |
| CHESTER: | *(Whispered)* Are they talking about us? |
| MICHAEL: | *(Whispered even lower)* Who else? |
| CHESTER: | *(Whispered)* What do we do? It sounds like they've got Dorothy and Sylvia out there. |
| MICHAEL: | *(Whispered)* Rescue them, of course. |
| CHESTER: | *(Whispered)* How? |

I had to admit it was a good question. I had no idea.

| | |
|---|---|
| VOICE 1: | Let's go in there and get them. |
| VOICE 3: | We'd better wait for the marshal. |
| VOICE 1: | You afraid of them? |
| VOICE 4: | Let's get them. You watch these two. |
| VOICE 3: | Right. I'll watch the girls. You go in and get them. |

There was a clatter of feet approaching the door. Chester and I flattened ourselves against the wall as the door opened. We stayed hidden by the open door while the angry crowd clattered by.

"What now?" Chester whispered.

"We split. Come on." I went around the door and out into the main room. Chester was right behind me.

Sylvia and Dorothy were in straight-back chairs in the center of the room. A thin, wizened little man, who I remembered was named Falkenburg, stood over them holding a broom. "Have you got them?" he asked.

"Got them," I snarled, "we *are* them."

He raised the broom as I ran toward them. "Don't you touch me. Help! Help!"

"Come on," I called to the girls. "Let's get out of here."

Sylvia butted the little man in the stomach before I could reach him, and he sat down on the floor with a surprised look on his face and no air in his lungs. We raced through the room and out to the corridor. We had almost made it to the stairs before the baying of the hounds started behind us. Down the stairs, past startled chambermaids and early-rising guests, we made it to the lobby. The sounds of pursuit increased behind us.

"Stop them! Halt! Grab them, somebody!"

"Yo! Tarrah! Yoiks! After the fiends!"

"Ouch! Get off my foot!"

"There they go—out the door. Get them!"

Chester, suiting word to need, had picked up the cry, further confusing the people we passed. "Stop!" he yelled, waving at nobody in front of us. "You can't get away with it! Evil will out! Halt! Desist! Birch, birch!"

Then we were out on the street, running. The question—which I didn't have enough breath left to ask—was, what next? Sylvia and Dorothy were skipping right along beside us, in much better shape than either Chester or I. It was still early enough so that the streets were deserted except for us and the madding crowd close behind.

Chester yelled, "Quick . . ."

MARP

"What?" Our friends were only about twenty yards behind, and closing fast. A loud blast of sound from somewhere ahead had cut off Chester's words.

". . . must take off all our . . ." MARP

"What?"

"Take off your clothes!"

MARP MARP PHEEEP

"What?"

"Why?"                    MARP

"Hurry, [MARP PHEEEEEEP] ask questions. [MARP] later. Just do it. Take off all your clothes." Chester ripped off his jacket, still running, and flung it to the side, then started struggling with his vest.

"I see," Sylvia yelled. "Of [MARP] course." She stripped the buttons from the front of her dress, gathered the skirt around her head and lifted. For a moment she looked like a fleet-footed crimson flower with a slim, white stem.

"SYLVIA!" Dorothy yelped. "What *are* you doing?" It seemed to be the first thing about the morning's proceedings that had upset her.

"Disrobing, Dorothy dear," Sylvia panted, leaving her petticoat to settle in the dust behind her.

"Well!" Dorothy yelled.

"You do it too," Sylvia called.

"Well. It certainly will cut down wind resistance," Dorothy yelled back. She did a sort of quick double-turn without cutting her running speed, and somehow had divested herself of her dress. Her outer and under garments seemed to be somehow connected, as they all came off as a unit and she continued down the street unadorned and fleet as a young, white-skinned gazelle.

"Now," Chester called, "just stop running and take everything else off." He sat down on the curb and started on his shoes and socks. "You too, Theodore Bear."

I was, I noticed, the only one with any substantial amount of clothing still on. I had ripped off my jacket, but was hesitating about my trousers. Not from any residual modesty, but because of a two-part problem. Part one: how to manage the technical maneuver of divesting myself of pants while in full flight. I hadn't seen how Chester managed it; I was watching Sylvia. Part two: I had a strong reluctance to give up the contents of my pants pockets. After all, you could never tell when a bunch of credit cards and a set of keys to an apartment that didn't even exist in this time line would come in handy. I have an innate reluctance to part with anything I've had with me for a long time. I still have my very own appendix.

The Horde was approaching. Chester and the girls were just about devoid of clothing, and it looked like I had become the mob's target. I stopped running and whipped off pants and shirt, tripping in the process and ending up flat on my back in the street, wrapped in a tangle of cloth.

"Quick," Chester yelled, "do something obscene!" He grabbed Dorothy by the hands and pulled her up and started prancing about in the street like an overweight frog. After a few seconds of panic Dorothy realized what was happening and joined in the dance: the gazelle and frog gavotte, for mixed pairs.

Sylvia raced to my aid, pulling off my shoes and socks and unravelled me from my clothes. "My," she said, "the life of a circus girl certainly gets interesting sometimes. Kiss me."

I did. Her lips tasted of honey: Wild thyme honey.

Our pursuers had reached us now, but they didn't seem to know it. They milled around for a while looking for us while we danced amongst them, and then split up into different groups and went off in various directions to find us. My foot was stepped on three times while they searched.

"Very clever, I grant you," I told Chester, as we sat on the edge of the sidewalk watching the last of the mob rigidly marching off into the distance. "A touch, a distinct touch. I'm glad it worked. Like you said, there are none so blind . . ."

"The second monkey," Chester said. "See no evil."

"I'm chilly," Dorothy said. "Can we put our clothes on now?"

"What next?" Sylvia asked. "That was fun."

"We gather up our clothes," Chester said, fishing under the sidewalk ledge for his shoe, "and get on board that train before they bring out the bloodhounds or something equally as drastic."

"Right. What train?"

"The train that was going Meep at us a few minutes ago."

"I should have guessed," I said. "And you're right: whatever else we're going to do, we'd better do it away from here."

"Excuse me for a minute," Sylvia said. She got up and headed across the street.

"Where are you going?" I asked.

"If we're going to take a train, there's something I should do before I get dressed."

"I won't even ask," I assured her retreating, er, back.

While she was gone Chester, Dorothy and I got dressed. Our clothes were trampled a bit from being walked on, but otherwise fine. Sylvia was back inside of three minutes and dressed inside of four, but I had my memories.

The train turned out to be four cars and a coal-burning engine, complete with cowcatcher and high-hat smokestack. As we walked into the red-brick stationhouse, the train pulled out.

"Come on," Chester said, breaking into a trot.

"There'll be another," I told him. "Running is undignified."

"There they are!" someone yelled from across the platform. "Let's get them!"

We ran. Without too much trouble we caught up with the last car and pulled and pushed each other aboard. A small black cloud of runners behind us gave up the chase a few seconds later and just stood there shaking their fists and yelling at the retreating train.

The conductor came out onto the pack platform with us, blue uniform neatly pressed and brass buttons shiny. "What," he asked, speaking as if he was afraid his mutton-chop whiskers would fall off if he wiggled his face too much, "do those persons on the track want?"

"They came to see us off, my good man," Chester pomped at him. "Our former students, they are. A bit of jolly fun."

"Bouncy, I call it. Distinctly bouncy. Tickets please."

"Ah, yes," Chester said, feeling about the pockets of his vest, "tickets, of course." He was doing his W. C. Fields bit. "Tickets. Yars. I believe, my good man, that we have left them beside our seats. If you will allow me . . ." He tried to shoulder his way past the conductor.

"You haven't any seats," the conductor pointed out "You just got on board. I saw you running for the train."

"Yars. That's true. How silly of me to have made such a mistake. I wonder what I could have done with the tickets." Chester turned to me. "Melvin, my lad, perchance did I give you the pasteboards to hold for me? I disremember what I did with the ducats."

"No, Uncle Hiram," I said. "I haven't seen them."

"Could be," the conductor suggested, "you never bought no tickets nohow. Could be."

"I think that's it, Uncle," Sylvia said sweetly. Chester turned to glare at her. "Here," she told him, pulling a packet from her decolletage, "is the money you asked me to hold for the tickets."

"I did?" Chester asked. "I mean, I am? You have?" He took the wad of money that Sylvia was thrusting at him and turned to the conductor. "I, ah, seem to have been mistaken. We have not, as of yet, purchased our tickets. Here, my good man; remove the correct sum from this petty cash and leave us be."

Eying us suspiciously, the conductor took his time in sorting out the required amount from the roll of bills. Then he handed what was left of the roll back to Chester and reached into his back pocket for the ticket book. Opening the worn, black leather case, he carefully selected four tickets and slowly unfolded them to their full eight-foot lengths. With his punch poised, he stood regarding the tickets. "All the way?" he demanded. We nodded. In a sudden tympani of motion, he put about eight punches in each ticket and handed the bunch to Chester. "I suppose," he said mournfully, "y'll be wanting receipts."

"No, thank you. We shall not require them."

The conductor wasn't going to get caught that way. "I'll have 'm for you in a second," he announced, continuing to firmly block the door. With a square, thick-tipped pencil, he proceeded to write our four unintelligible documents on four copies of an all-purpose form. The form was ruled off into six areas, which he filled in with a combination of demotic writing and astrological diagrams. Each area had a printed heading, as follows:

1. Name of Passenger or Type of Livestock
2. Destination or Cause of Disturbance
3. Yardage, Roughage, Breakage or Cost of Dinner
4. Estivation or Religion
5. Excuse
6. Disposition: [*check one*]
                accepted [ ] rejected [ ] eaten [ ]

"Thank you," Chester said, taking the forms. "I can't tell you how much we appreciate all you've done for us."

"Only my parameter," the conductor stated, and went back inside the car.

"Well," I said, watching the little dot that was the town of West Mutton recede into the horizon line. "We made it, so far."

Chester rolled the thirty-two feet of tickets and thrust them deep into a jacket pocket. "God is just," he said.

"Just what?" I asked.

"Just watching."

Sylvia held my arm. "Let's go inside," she said. "It's . . ."

# BLIP

# 5

I t felt like an earthquake hitting a rollercoaster. We were all thrown against the guardrail and then back against the inside door. The floor bucked and heaved. A loud screeching was almost drowned out by what sounded like the inside of a waterfall. I clung as hard as I could to the large emergency brake wheel and Sylvia had one arm around my left arm and the other around my neck. Chester was kind of sideways, spread out against the guardrail, with Dorothy wrapped around one leg.

The screeching stopped. The waterfall sound continued while the railroad car tilted, lifting the platform we were on high in the air. It poised there long enough for all sound to stop, and then fell back down with a crash that jarred my back teeth.

Then the screaming started. The passengers inside the car discovered that something unusual had happened, and reacted in that calm, rational manner that separates *Homo sapiens* from the lesser creatures. They sat there and yelled.

"What was all that?" Chester asked. "Was anyone hurt?"

"I think I'm all right, or I will be as soon as I catch my breath. A few bruises, that's all," Dorothy said.

"Urph," I said helpfully. "We've blipped again."

"I think I'm going to be sick," said Sylvia weakly. "No, I guess I'm not, I just feel as if I should be."

"Later," Chester said. "We haven't got time now."

"What more do you expect to happen?" I asked.

"I don't know, but I don't think we should be here when those people come out of the train."

"I don't think they'll bother us."

Chester nodded. "So. Tell me, do you think they'll *help* us?"

"A point," I conceded. "Let's split."

"Did you notice," Chester asked, "that the time has changed again? It's just about dusk. The sun seems to have just set."

I climbed over the rail and leaped heavily to the ground. "That," I called up to him, "ain't all. I know why we cracked up."

"Why?" Dorothy asked, peering over the side.

"Because there isn't any rail here. We've come to a time track in which they haven't invented the train. Here, let me help you down." I helped Dorothy and Sylvia over the edge of the car, and then Chester appeared, looking down.

"Step aside," he said. "I'll jump."

"Careful you don't break a leg."

Without even bothering to give me a withering glance, he leaped lightly to the ground. "Perhaps they just didn't build their railroads in the same places," he offered. "It's probably just as well. Instead of running out of track, we might have collided with an us-bound freight. Let's make our way out of here while there's still enough light to see where we're going."

We walked steadily away from the trackless train, where yells of authority were starting to replace cries of anguish. We were in a wide grass and bush area between two forests. Those who still maintain that the human animal is born without instincts could try to explain for me the reason why we headed, without discussion, for the nearer forest rather than trying either direction of the grassy lane we were in.

"Look," Sylvia said, pointing into the gloom of the forest to our left. "Somebody waves."

We changed our direction slightly and headed toward the waving hand. There, beneath the shelter of a great and ancient tree on the border between field and forest, sat five people in a close semicircle. A sixth, a teen-age girl in rags of Lincoln green, stood behind them waving to us with arms rigid like a boyscout trying for his merit badge in signals.

The seated five made an interesting display. In the center, cross-legged, sat a man of indeterminate age, thinning hair neatly combed straight back, drooping walrus moustache, wearing an air of elaborate concern for arcane ritual. He was dressed in a black jacket and vest of musty origin, dungaree pants, an off-white shirt with a square collar from which protruded a string bowtie, and no shoes.

On the far left, kneeling and bowed over, with his head touching the ground, a youth wearing red shorts and a poncho was trying to make music by blowing through a blade of grass. The girl next to him, dressed in a red velvet undershirt and not much past the age of budding, was beating time to the grass music, her palms paradiddling on her thigh.

On the far right, a short girl in a long, gold evening gown sat with her legs tucked under her. She had a round face, framed by long, carrot-red hair, and the practiced air of a pixie. At the moment, she was taking a deep drag from a long-stemmed pipe, her eyes crossed inward in concentration on the glowing bowl. Near right, a girl who couldn't be more than eight years old dozed peacefully, her head resting securely in the pixie's lap.

At our approach, the central figure looked up from a globe on the grass before him that he had been studying, and reflexively buttoned his jacket. "Greetings," he said. "Are you from the miraculous trolley out yonder?"

"We, ah, were passengers on the train, yes." Chester answered.

"Welcome passengers. Sit with us and partake of our pipeweed."

"Pipeweed?" Chester sounded interested.

"Homegrown. The very best. Ceremonial."

"Well," Chester said, producing his brass pipe with the aplomb of a magician. "I believe I might, just might, be interested."

The other members of the group were regarding us with all of the interest that might be given to a new butterfly, but the pipeweed man and the semaphore girl had found new friends. The girl came shyly around to the front of the group. "Hello," she said. "I'm Marian-Made."

"Hello," I said. "I'm Michael the Theodore Bear. These are Chester, Sylvia and Dorothy. It's a pleasure to meet you, Maid Marian."

The pipeweed man smiled widely, displaying gapped teeth. "I think I'd better do the introductions, for the sake of confusion."

To prevent, I wondered, or induce.

"The gentleman to our far right, your left," he said, indicating the grass-playing lad, who did not look up, "is Marian." He handed a small leather pouch to Chester, who filled his pipe from its contents. "This young lady, the newest member of our group, is Marian-Made. She took the name after her first night here. We all take new names when we join the group.

"I," he tapped himself on the tie, "am Tom. Tom Bombadil, at your service. The lady to my left, your right, is Goldberry." She smiled and passed him the pipe, being careful not to disturb the sleeping child.

"Oh," I said brightly. "Have you read *Lord of the Rings?*"

"I don't read," Bombadil said. "The Lady Goldberry reads. She picked our names when we started the group. Says they fit. Mine seemed to fit me without a strain, so I wear it." He took a deep pull from the pipe, seeming very pleased with himself.

"This," Goldberry said, smiling down at the sleeping child, "is our daughter. We call her Nobody."

An ego-building name if I've ever heard one.

Chester pulled his gas lighter out and applied fire to the proper end of his pipe in a foot-long burst of flame. He had his lighter adjusted to light cigarettes across the room. It was his favorite parlor trick. He nodded gravely twice and waved the pipe in my direction before sitting slowly down on the soft grass. His ears turned slowly red, and then the flush continued over his face.

I took the pipe and sniffed. Pipeweed had the aroma of the finest Moroccan Mauve. I inhaled. It was strong stuff.

Chester released his breath in a sudden cough. The redness diffused and disappeared from his face as quickly as it had come. "Pipeweed," he mused. "There's a market for pipeweed. That is, if we ever again find a place where there's a market."

The girl who had been beating on her thigh stopped and turned slowly, to look at Chester. Her wide-open eyes, framed behind a pair of great, round-lensed, wire-framed glasses, stared unblinkingly. "There is a market," she said hesitantly, as though she were groping not so much for words as for the very concept of language. "There is a large market. It is over that way." She pointed. "In that direction. If you walk you will come to it. It is only a few hills away. A super-market is it." She stopped pointing.

"That's Owl," Bombadil said. "She knows."

"What?" Chester asked. "What does she know?"

"What she has learned."

The girl had a curious tense look, as though she were mentally straining for something, but unable to reach it.

Sylvia went over to her and sat down, "Hello," she said, gently reaching out her hand. "Hello, Owl."

Owl took the outstretched hand in both of hers and squeezed tightly. "It doesn't sell pipeweed," she said.

"What's that?" Sylvia asked softly.

The girl turned her big eyes toward Sylvia. "The market," she explained. "It doesn't sell pipeweed. That's why we have to grow our own. Besides, we haven't any money anymore. Any of us. Any money. Any. Hello."

"She's our computer," Bombadil explained. "She has all the information somewhere inside of her. Ask her something."

"Like what?" Chester asked, intrigued.

"Anything, like. Just anything. You'll see."

Chester shrugged—his full-length, which involves arms, hands and fingers along with shoulders. "Right. Who was the third president of the United States?"

Owl continued staring at Sylvia.

"Owl!" Bombadil said, clapping his hands. "You see," he asided to Chester, "she's the computer, but you might consider me the programmer. I know how to get it out of her. It's a knack. Owl, listen. Turn on. Presidents—got that? Presidents. American presidents. You know the American presidents?"

"Isn't it funny," Owl asked Sylvia, "that America has vice-presidents, but it doesn't have any special presidents for anything else?"

"It's like plotting a graph," Bombadil told us. "That's the first line; now for the intersection. Owl, number the presidents. One, two, three; like that. I want three."

"One," Owl said, with no change in her voice. "George Washington. Inaugurated 1789, he served eight years. He died on December 14, 1799. Two: John Adams. Served four years from 1797 and died on the fourth of July in 1826. Thomas Jefferson was three. From 1801, he served eight years. He died on the same day as John Adams. Funny, there was another president who died on the fourth of July: number five, James Monroe. He served eight years from 1817, and died July fourth, 1831. Two other presidents died the same day of the year: Millard Fillmore and William Howard Taft. That was March eighth. Both presidents who died in September were assassinated: James A. Garfield on the seventeenth, and William McKinley on the fourteenth. No American president has died during the month of May."

"Enough!" Bombadil said sharply. "Sometimes," he told Chester, "she gets sidetracked. But she knows it all; the trick is to get it out of her. I'm getting good at it. Try something else."

"How did she get so smart?" Chester asked. The girl was still staring with her big eyes into Sylvia's, paying no attention to the rest of us.

"When she was on hype she got on to a reading kick. Went through the town library in three days. Then she went through the Library of Congress microfilm file by telecall. It almost killed her till she came down. She couldn't forget anything and had instant recall and access, what they call it. Now she's down."

"Hype?" I asked.

"Yah, yah. You know: superspeed. Betterphet. Hype. Don't you know it? You guys aren't rights men, are you?" "I never would have guessed."

"No, we're not whatever," I assured him.

"That's good. Not that it matters, I mean. If I had any stuff I'd lay it on you, but hell, not a pill under this tree. Just the natural grass. Ask her something."

Chester turned to me. "You," he said. "You're the history freak; pick a date."

It seemed to me that Bombadil was showing Owl off the way a preteen shows off a new toy, and I don't think that anyone should own someone else's mind. But I seldom have the courage of my convictions until they're ready to bite. "Kings," I said, "of England. Name them."

Bombadil swiveled to face Owl and slapped his palms sharply together. "The English. Owl, do you hear? The English. Can you name their kings?"

"Kings?" Owl asked quietly, as though not quite sure what was wanted.

"The English kings," Bombadil stated. "Name them!"

"The English kings," Owl said blankly. "The House of Cerdic. Ecgberth, from 802 to 837. Then the brothers, Athelbald, Althelberth, Athelred, and Alfred, known as the Cake, one after the other till 901. Then Edward the Elder till 925; Athelstan to 940; Edmund to 946; and Edred to 955. Then Edwig, son of Edmund and his wife Alfgifu, to 959 and his brother Edgar to 975. Edward the Martyr to 979; when his half-brother Ethelred the Unready took over to reign till 1016. Edmund Ironside from April 23 to November 30, 1016. Cnut, who married Emma of Normandy, widow of Ethelred the Unready, ruled from 1017 to 1035. Harold the Bastard from 1035 to 1040, and Harthacnut, his half-brother and not a bastard, to 1042. Then Edward the Confessor from 1042 to 1066." She paused.

"Go on," Bombadil urged.

"Those are the English kings." Her voice was flat.

"It could be said," I offered, "that the line of English kings stopped in 1066. As a matter of fact, it has been said."

Tom Bombadil inspected me suspiciously. One who had opinions on the legitimacy of the Norman Conquest would, obviously, bear close watching. One who could count over five and who didn't use it as a parlor trick would bear similar attention.

"Something else," he insisted. "Ask her something else."

"I don't think so," I said.

"Let's leave her alone," Chester added.

"Just one more time. Come on. Ask her something else. She's like a computer, all full of facts and stuff if you know how to get it out."

"How does she feel about it?" I asked.

Bombadil stared at us. The question had no meaning for him.

Chester tried. "Does she want to answer all these questions?"

"Man, she wants to be stoned and I keep her stoned. That's what she wants."

"That's all?"

"Man, what else *is* there?" He looked puzzled for a moment, then relaxed. "Go ahead, ask her something else—anything."

"Owl," Sylvia said clearly and tenderly, "tell me, who are you?"

"Huh?" Bombadil said.

Owl stared intently at Sylvia, and her eyes grew big behind her glasses. She started sobbing softly, as a small baby does when it thinks no one will answer if it cries out loud.

"I'm here, Owl," Sylvia told her, holding firmly on to her hands.

"Say," Bombadil said. "What are you people doing to her? She's never cried before."

"Would it have done any good before?" Chester asked.

"What good does crying do? I used to cry all the time, and it never got me nothing."

"Excuse me," Dorothy interrupted, "do any of you happen to know what that thing is? That thing up there." She pointed to the sky above the meadow and we all looked.

The flying saucer was back: blue and red lights, whistle, honk and all. The funny thing was that I didn't hear the thing until after Dorothy pointed it out. It was something like turning around and discovering that a brass band playing "The Stars and Stripes Forever" has snuck up behind you.

"I don't know," Goldberry said, smiling, "but it was here yesterday and it ate somebody."

"Ate somebody?" Chester asked.

Bombadil nodded. "I saw it too. That's the best way to describe it. There was a kid in the middle of the field doing his thing, which happened to be digging square holes in the ground and putting orange crates with circles cut out of the top over them to make individual latrines. He'd been doing it for a couple of days; got quite a row of them. Maybe twenty-five, thirty. Your choo-choo must have run right over them. Anyway, he was digging away at this latrine when all of a sudden that thing honked. I mean like, one second it wasn't there and the next, there it was. Honking. He looked up, this kid I mean, and started running away from it. It buzzed straight to him, swooped down, and he wasn't there anymore. Gulp. Then it flew away."

"That's cute," I said. "Think it's after us?"

"No," Chester said. "It's after them." He nodded. The people who had been in the train were all gathered in a group. I guess they were talking about what happened and what to do next. The saucer was stalking them the way a boy stalks bullfrogs.

The people spread out before the honking saucer; running, panicked, in all directions like bullfrogs escaping from a pond. The saucer darted this way and that, unable to make a decision; then it swooped down once, twice, thrice, gulping up one or two people with each swoop and darting off into the distance. The whole operation couldn't have taken more than ninety seconds.

"Like that" Bombadil said. "Just like that." The sound of screaming reached us from the nearest survivors, who were still running.

Chester stood up, dusted himself off and put the toke-pipe carefully back in his pocket. "Thank you for your hospitality," he said. "I really think we must be going now."

"Now?" Dorothy repeated. "Shouldn't we wait here to make sure that thing is gone?"

"Right now," Chester said firmly.

"Where are you going?" Bombadil asked.

Chester considered. Then he pointed. "That way."

"Okay," Bombadil said with a large shrug. "Do your thing."

"We have to go now," Sylvia told Owl, who was silently watching her. "Are you all right?"

"Yes."

"Take care of yourself."

"Yes. Yes. I shall. I will. You also, take care." Owl smiled.

The four of us walked off into the gathering darkness in the direction Chester had pointed. In a short time we were surrounded by trees.

"I hope you know what you're doing," I said, stumbling over a root.

"Have no fear," Chester said. "Ouch!"

"It's pitch black," I said, "Shouldn't we at least wait until daylight?"

"Just a little further," Chester said.

Dorothy called, "Where are you?" She sounded quite close, but I couldn't see her.

"Over here," I called.

She made her way over, banging first into Sylvia and then into me. I told her, "You must have very poor night vision."

"Nonsense," she insisted. "I can see that it's nighttime as well as anybody. If we must keep on, why don't we rope ourselves together, or at least hold hands?"

"Come on, take my hand. It would further us to be farther away from that field when the UFO returns."

"You think it's coming back?" I asked.

"It did once. That's not the only reason I wanted to get us away from there, but it's a good one."

"I'll grant you that."

"It would further and faster us to hold hands," Sylvia said.

"Yes," Chester said. "I think I've found a road, or at least a path."

We walked along the Chester-found path Indian-file, Chester in the lead (it was his path), holding hands and not talking. Each of us was too deep in his own thoughts and too busy trying not to trip to carry on a conversation. The first words in about half an hour came from Dorothy. "Enough," she said.

Chester stopped. Dorothy banged into him, I bumped into Dorothy, and Sylvia walked into me. "Enough (oof) what?" he asked.

"Enough walking. Let us sit down and rest for a while. This leading and being led is very tiring."

"All right," Chester agreed. "Let's get off the road a little way and sit down. We'll take a ten-minute break."

# 6

When I woke up, the sun was rising over my left arm. Over my right arm, chest and most of my back sprawled Sylvia, her eyes closed tight in sleep. Chester and Dorothy were already up and were busy setting fire to a small bunch of twigs and leaves. I rolled over carefully, so as not to wake Sylvia, and sat up. "Morning."

"Indeed," Chester grouched. "Any other comments or observations you'd care to make?"

"Sorry," I said pleasantly. "I should know better than to try to talk to you before you've had coffee in the morning. What's the fire for?"

"I'm planning to be rescued by a brown bear in a ranger's cap," Chester explained.

"We're making coffee," Dorothy volunteered.

"That would help," I admitted. I got up and stretched my cramped bones. "Where did we get the coffee to make?"

"I always carry disposacups," Dorothy said. "When you work in a circus you travel a lot." She finished her project of erecting a forked stick over the fire and carefully set a can of water in the fork.

"You lug around the water too?"

"I fetched the water," Chester said. "There's a stream down there," he pointed, "and a pile of empty tin cans by the stream. Modern man strikes again. 'By their works ye shall know them.' Ancient Latin saying. The Latins were an uncivilized tribe who conquered the world but left behind no tin cans to mark their passage."

"They would have if they'd had the cans to leave behind."

"Cynic."

"You'll feel better after you've had your coffee."

Dorothy opened her shoulderbag and took out four flat, round disks of paper. She squeezed the sides, and the disks popped out into paper cups. "Can you take the can off the fire?" she asked.

"Sure," I told her. "But I don't know if I can pour it." I rolled my jacket around my hands and took the can of boiling water carefully out of the fork.

"Just set it down," Dorothy said. "Chester wanted to boil the water before we use it for sanitary reasons. The cups are self-heating."

When the tin was cool enough to pour from, Dorothy filled the cups. About five seconds later each of them was boiling again.

Sylvia sat up. "Coffee!" she said. "Is our ten-minute rest over?"

Chester groaned.

After coffee we went down to Chester's stream to wash. It was too cold and shallow for serious bathing, but a few splashes in the face did as much as the coffee to wake me up. Then we gathered together for a council meeting.

"Well," I said to Chester, "what next?"

"We need a plan," he announced.

Dorothy asked, "Why?"

Chester groped in the air in front of him for words to express his thoughts. "If you're lost in the woods and you're not very careful to go in a straight line, you'll go around in a big circle until you starve to death. A plan is our way of going in a straight line. Almost any plan, as long as it's consistent."

"Okay," I agreed. "Pick a plan."

"Let's consult the *I Ching* for a plan. That's what it's best at."

"Fine," I agreed. "Go ahead. It's your turn anyway."

"What's an Itching?" Sylvia asked.

I explained as best I could. She volunteered to give me her birth date and rising sign if it would help, and I explained some more.

Chester squatted on the earth and threw his coins. "A lot of moving lines: many changes. There. Let's see. *Ken* under *K'un*. Fifteen: Modesty. Changing to sixty: Limitation." He slid the tube out of his pocket and squinted toward the sun. "Yes. Well, well, well."

"What is it?" Dorothy asked.

Chester put his viewing tube away and stood up. "We must continue, that's all. It's all in how you interpret it."

"I'll bite," I said. "How do you interpret it?"

"Enough talk. Onward! Come on, let's get going."

"Okay. Okay. Don't push."

Dorothy strode up to Chester, who was taking the lead along the trail. "Very good," she said. "Tell me, have you ever considered becoming a ringmaster?"

"I dreamed about Adolphus last night," Sylvia told me. "He's fine, and well, and we will find him."

"I hope you're right," I said.

"She has this affinity," Dorothy said. "One time she dreamed that Adolphus was badly frightened, so she woke up in a panic and ran over to the animal tent. A snake had broken loose and was in Adolphus's stall. The poor beast was so frightened that it couldn't even whinny. She just picked the snake up and put it back in its cage. Five feet of python."

We went along silently for a time, while I practiced looking at Sylvia with a new respect. Then the trail intersected an asphalt road.

"Civilization," Chester declared.

I shrugged. "It's just a road."

"Yes, but there's a tire over there. Civilization."

"Hist!" Sylvia said. "Someone comes—I hear clinking."

"Clinking?"

A second later I could hear the clinking. Then the clinkers came into view. Six men in leather pants and iron suits walked around the corner.

"Spanish conquistadors!" Chester said.

"Italians," I volunteered. "Fourteenth-century Italian knights."

"The Queen's Guards!" Dorothy exclaimed. "We're home!"

"They're not the Guards, Dorothy," Sylvia said. "And I think they're drunk." They were indeed weaving and staggering down the road toward us.

*"Ars grabbis!"* the one in the lead shouted, seeing us. He turned back to his companions. *"Leavis protamis! Hic! Yatta lo fraturntitti up."*

*"Too too papilarus,"* one of his companions agreed, leaning against a tree.

*"Bashmire!"* another exclaimed.

We stood by the side of the road, unsure whether we should stay or run, laugh or cry, as the horseless knights approached. Chester raised his hand. "Welcome, good friends," he called.

"Congratulations," I whispered out of the side of my mouth. "That's three assumptions in as many words; I think you've set a record."

"Shut up," Chester whispered back.

*"Grap fikker toom?"* the lead tinman called. *"Grabul fram?"*

I stepped forward. "Every other Thursday," I told him. "Except when the lead guitar is sick. Three cents a yard, wrapped."

The six of them clanked to a stop about ten yards away. They spent ten or fifteen seconds eying us the way some people look at hamburger, then went into a huddle.

"I don't like this," I told Chester.

"You shouldn't have insulted them," he said. "Girls, stand behind us."

"How could they have been insulted if they didn't understand what I said?"

"It's your attitude," Chester explained.

One of the tinmen kept breaking out of the huddle, turning around to glare at us, and then going back. I felt like the center in an unfriendly football game. Or, possibly, the ball.

There was a cracking sound behind me, and I looked around to find Dorothy trimming the twigs off a good-sized branch. "Do you know anything about quarterstaff buffeting?" she asked.

"I've seen Robin Hood in the movies," I said. "And a couple of those Japanese cutemups. But I've never tried it myself."

"In my youth," Dorothy said, coming alongside us with her six-foot chopstick, "I was woman's champion of New Lincolnshire."

"Do you remember much of it?" I asked.

She glared at me. "That was four months ago."

"Sorry. I guess I'd better do something about arming myself." I searched around for a club. The first hunk of wood I picked up had been lying there too long; it broke in half when I lifted it. The second, a hefty three-foot section was fresh and sturdy.

"Is that not a mite short?" Dorothy asked me.

I told her, "The Romans conquered the world with three-foot swords."

"I presume they had edges and points," she said.

"I'll do my best without," I said. "Or would you like to sharpen this?"

"Don't fight before a battle," Chester said firmly. "It would seem that Dorothy can take care of herself. If anything starts, watch out for Sylvia."

"I think you missed the point of the story I told earlier," Dorothy said. "Sylvia can take care of herself better than any of us."

Sylvia stood, slim and defenseless, by the side of the road. I had gotten into this to take care of her, and was going to do my best. I moved over until I was between her and the opposition. She might be able to take care of herself better than any of us, but she wasn't going to have to prove it if I could help it.

Chester stood with his hands in his pockets and looked annoyed. "I don't think they like us," he said.

The six of them broke off the huddle and turned to face us in squad formation. The leader, in left-middle position, raised his hand. *"Huggem squamish aye lipto!"* he called. He pointed to the two girls. *"Huggem squamish!"* he repeated, making a beckoning motion. He pointed to Chester and me. *"Backem rapish,"* he said, with a go-away gesture.

With a further series of words and obscene gestures he indicated that he wanted the girls to do with as he and his men had read about in all those nasty books back in the barracks. Chester and I should just go away. Otherwise they'd simply kill us and take the girls anyway.

Dorothy turned her staff sideways and hefted it. The soldiers seemed to think this was very funny.

"Rape and looting," I said to Chester. "That's all these army types think about, rape and looting. It's disgraceful."

"Lack of team athletics," Chester commented. "They ought to play more volleyball."

"Aren't you going to arm yourself?" I asked him.

"I am armed. Legged too, for that matter. If things look bad, remember that we can probably outrun them. They must be carrying easily thirty pounds of armor each."

"I'll keep it in mind," I assured him.

The troops decided that we weren't going to leave peacefully and resigned themselves to chopping us apart. The ends each leveled pikes at us, and the rest of the line drew their swords. Three and a half feet of single-edge, badly tempered steel. They started advancing slowly, keeping in line.

"Michael," Sylvia asked, "are they serious?"

"I would say so," I told her. No use lying about something she'd find out in three or four minutes anyway.

"And would you say they're trained soldiers?"

"Well, at any rate they've practiced a bit. Don't worry," I said, spreading artificial confidence, "we'll take care of them."

"I'm not worried," Sylvia assured me. "I just didn't want to hurt them if there was any chance they'd go away and leave us alone."

"What?" I said. But I was suddenly too preoccupied to demand a further explanation of her comment. The line of tin-clad infantry broke into a trot and swept down at us.

We stood there, frozen for a long moment, and then all hell broke loose. All hell, in this case, was mostly Sylvia. I felt her hands on my shoulders, pushing up. And then her feet. And then she had launched herself at the lead soldier like a snow leopard taking a sheep.

With a startled cry, the commander brought his sword up to defend himself from this unexpected attack. Sylvia pulled knees and shoulders together into a tight, spinning ball of trained muscle and then snapped out. The commander's sword whistled as he pulled it down to meet this new threat, but too late. With all the momentum of her leap, Sylvia's arms and shoulders met the ground and acted as springs to transfer the energy to the other tip of her body—her legs, which with piston-like speed drove forward and up to their point of impact. Her feet met the commander's chin with a sound like a pistol shot, and his head snapped back; instantly breaking his neck. He fell like a pile of tin cans.

Sylvia stood over his body like a goddess: slim, lithe, innocent, beautiful and terrible as uncaged lightning; and there was an unholy look in her eyes.

By this time, line had met line, and the battle was engaged. One of the pikemen tried to push Dorothy aside so she wouldn't be hurt and could be saved for later sport. With a left-hand twist of her staff she knocked the pike up, and then brought the staff under and in. It caught the pikeman right below the cuirass and drove deep into a sensitive spot. He dropped to the ground, clutching himself and gasping for breath.

A swordsman came at me, and I parried his lunge with my club. He swung a few more times, but I held him off easily. I couldn't get at him and he seemed satisfied to stand there swinging at me. Then I realized: every time I parried his swing a chip flew off my club. In another minute he would have cut it in half; this would never do. I lunged at him, forcing him to take a step backward. He yammered some invective and changed his tactics, thrusting point-first at my chest. I just barely caught the point on my club. He pulled back, and the club was almost yanked out of my hand.

He was as startled as I was: the point of his sword had driven tightly into the club and wouldn't pull free. *"Yargha!"* he yelled, jerking the sword from side to side. But now I had the advantage—for as long as that sword stayed stuck. He could only hold the sword by the hilt, but I had the leverage of the whole club. I grabbed the club at both ends and twisted. He struggled fiercely to hold on to the sword as it twisted in his hands. With a sudden heave, which cost me my balance, I yanked the sword from his grasp and fell backward. Club and sword flew over my head and into the brush. My opponent drew a long, spade-shaped dirk from its scabbard and lunged at me. I rolled and kicked, catching him across the knee, then scrambled to my feet to avoid his next rush. He didn't make one. With his mouth opened in a vast O, and his face turned flour-white, he slowly toppled to the ground, his leg stiffly thrust before him. He was no longer aware of my presence. I had broken his kneecap, and he could think of nothing beyond his own pain.

Which, as it happens, was all right with me.

The three remaining heroes had all rushed Chester, who stood there, nonchalantly, his hands in his pockets. When the first one was about to reach him, he pulled his gas lighter out of his pocket and gushed two feet of flame from his outstretched arm. The flame formed a protective semicircle in front of him, as his hand weaved the lighter in an intricate pattern. The three tinmen stopped, startled, and poked gingerly at the flame with their weapons.

Dorothy, swinging her staff like a great baseball bat, floored the left-most one with her first blow. Sylvia leaped on the middle one from behind and pressed her thumbs into the sides of his neck, cutting off the blood to his brain. After three seconds he dropped, unconscious.

I took one bare-handed step toward the one man left standing with no clear idea of what to do about him. He looked around and saw the four of us closing in; Chester flipping the lighter on and off like a serpent's tongue licking in and out. After a moment's indecision he dropped his pike, turned and fled.

Dorothy looked around at our felled foes lying silent on the ground or writhing and moaning in the grass. "Shall we," she asked, hefting her six-foot twig, "put them out of their misery?"

"Dorothy!" Sylvia, looking very petite and innocent, sounded shocked. I remembered a quote about the female of the species, and tried to decide which of these two it most applied to.

"Let us walk, casually but rapidly, away from this scene of carnage," Chester suggested. "After all, they may have friends."

"Great idea," I agreed.

We headed down the asphalt in the opposite direction from that our vanquished foe had taken.

We had abluted at a convenient pump by an empty house, ministered as best we could to our surprisingly few bruises and scrapes, and were a few hours away from the battleground when the sound of pursuit came first to our—Sylvia's—ears. "Quick, off the road!" she exclaimed. "A galloping beast comes behind."

"What sort of beast?" Chester asked.

"One with hooves," she said.

"Just one?"

By this time we could all hear it: one horse clattering toward us. We clumped together on the side of the road, figuring one horse meant one man and we could handle one man.

As the rider approached, I had a very strong sense of *déjà vu*. A brown range pony at full gallop, carrying a lean man in tan buckskins. The rider leaning forward in his lightweight saddle, on tightly cinched stirrups, as if to urge the mount onward; reins lightly held in one hand with the other resting on the extra-large saddlebags behind. I had seen this all before.

Then I knew where. It was a scene out of American history: *The Pony Express,* starring Gary Cooper. I told Chester.

"Oyho! Oyho!" the rider yelled as he drew even with us. "Make way! In the name of the Empress! The Overland Mail!" And then he was past.

"It may well be a scene out of history," Chester remarked, staring at the retreating back, "but I'm afraid it isn't American history. He could probably tell us a fascinating story if we dragged him off his horse. Ah, well." We trudged on.


"Where," Dorothy asked in what I was coming to recognize as her argumentative voice, "are we going?"

Chester shrugged. "You pick a place."

There was no reply.

It was about time, I decided, for one of my famous funny stories. "Did I ever tell you," I inquired at random, "of the time we held an orgy on the Flushing local, and the lutist got a string caught in the . . ."

"I was there," Chester reminded me dourly.

"What's a flushing local?" Sylvia demanded.

"Look," I said. "Isn't that something in the road ahead?"

"How are you punctuating that?" Chester asked suspiciously.

"There," I insisted. "Look. It's a car."

When we were close I saw that the object was a car only in so far as form follows function. It had once been a car: a black, four-door gangster model, complete with running boards and spare tire mounted in the fender. It was now a hulk. Tires rotted off, headlights and windows broken, fenders and bumpers rusted through; the car was slowly going back to the earth from which it was mined.

On top of the car hulk a man, wrapped in a white sheet, sat cross-legged and stared serenely off at the horizon. He managed to subtly convey the impression that he'd been there as long as the car.

"Look," Chester said. "A guru."

Dorothy looked. "He's dirty," she said. "Is that why you call him ugh-aroo?"

"I think he's a Grand High Exalted Muckamuck in the KKK," I suggested.

Sylvia, as usual, took direct action. "Hello," she said, walking over to the side of the wreck. There was no response. "Please, sir, could you tell us where we are?"

The head riding above the pyramid of sheet slowly turned until the beard was facing Sylvia, then stopped. "You," it declared calmly, "are here."

"Aha," I said. "One of those; I knew it."

"Here," Chester offered, stepping forward. "Let me." He stood in front of the car and raised his hand, palm upward. "Greetings. Will you enlighten us?"

Whitesheet stared down at Chester for a long moment "Impossible," he declared.

Sylvia displayed patience. "Good sir," she said, standing on tiptoe and smiling brightly, "will you tell us what we will find further down the road?"

Whitesheet nodded. "Yes."

We waited.

"Perhaps," I suggested after three or four minutes had passed, "we should . . ."

"That way," Whitesheet said, flopping an arm out to his left, "lies madness."

Sylvia stared along a parallel to the pointing finger and considered the vista. "But," she noted, "there's no road."

"Most who seek manage to find their way. On the other hand," he raised his other hand, "over there be dragons. Or, at least, dragon."

He was indicating the direction we were heading.

"Oh!" Sylvia exclaimed. "Fierce, up-tight, fire-breathing dragons?"

"One young dragonette, her furnace barely stoked, and her brood of hatchlings."

"Thank you," Sylvia said.

"Dragons?" I asked Chester.

"Unicorns?" he replied.

During all of this Dorothy had been staring at the car-sitter with an expression of earnest curiosity. Finally she could no longer contain it. She rose. "You," she said, gesturing so that there could be no mistake as to whom she meant. "What are you doing up there?"

His head turned with the steady sweep of a radar beacon until his unblinking gaze was full on Dorothy, then stopped. "I," he stated in a voice that would brook no disagreement, "am the rightful King of France, with a strong claim on the thrones of Spain, Portugal, England, the Holy Roman—or, if you prefer, Austro-Hungarian—Empire, Italy, Greece, Mexico, the Duchies of Herzegovina, Faulkenberg, Ruritania, Alba, Courland, Bosnia, and others too numerous to mention. I have been done out of my heritage; and I'm going to sit right here until I get it back. My faithful minions are, even now, preparing the way."

Chester snorted. "You'll have to do better than that."

The radar gaze turned to him. "If I must. I am a student of the Mysteries of the East. After much meditation and study, I had perfected the technique of levitation; and while I was up here, five feet off the ground, somebody stuck an old car under me."

"That," Chester agreed, "is better."

I laughed. "Which are we to believe?"

"All three."

"Three?"

The radar eyes burned into mine from under bushy brows. "I came out here to do a character bit in a television commercial. The rest of the crew never showed up, and I'm staying till they do. At triple time. I've been here nine years now."

"Three," I agreed.

"Come on," Chester said, herding us around the car.

"Goodbye," the prince/guru/actor called as we walked down the road. "Watch out for dragon."

It was around the next bend. There was a clearing to the left of the road that was full of round, flat-top stones and had been roofed over with some sort of tenting material. The hatchlings were squatting, one to a stone, and clutching small slates. A strange squeaking sound that filled the air proved to be the four-foot upright alligators writing on the slates with hunks of chalk. In front of the group, at the far end of the clearing, eighteen feet of prime lady dragon paced back and forth, whipping a large tail in great arcs behind. "I said the next slide, please," she called out in a vibrato soprano bellow.

A small, harassed-looking man fiddled with a large black box in mid-clearing. "I'm trying, I'm trying," he replied nervously.

"Constantly," dragonette agreed. "Ah!" she sighed, breathing out just the tiniest wisp of flame, "there." After a clicking sound from either the man or the projector, a large picture was cast partly on her and mostly on a backdrop behind her.

Nobody had noticed us standing at the back edge of this outdoor classroom, and I thought it better to keep it that way. "What now?" I whispered to Chester. "Hide here until they go away—or, maybe until I wake up?"

"I refuse," Chester told me, "to be a figment of your dream. That lacks imagination. Besides, I know who'd get the best part."

"The question," I said. "I asked you a question; the least you can do is answer it."

"Yes. Well. I think the best thing we can do is walk quietly by. The only one in a position to notice us is Madam Teacher, and she's too busy."

"Interesting theory, friend," I said. "Would you care to be the first to make the experiment?"

"Come on, you've been a teacher. You know that you have to ignore petty problems so as not to disrupt the class. It would be better to be seen crossing by Teach up there than found hiding by the kids."

"Okay," I said. "I just hope it's not near lunch break." The four of us bunched together and proceeded to calmly (ha!) and quietly walk by the back of the clearing.

"This," dragonlady was saying, tapping the picture with a ten-foot pole, "is a famous illustration of one of the great stories of Dragonpast. Can any of you hatchlings tell me what it is?"

I looked as we passed. For a moment the shadings of light and shadow created a pattern that canceled the projection. Then my eye adjusted to the shade, and the picture was clear. It was the classic view of Saint George and the Dragon. You know the one: George on a rearing horse, his armor gleaming gold, about to plunge his lance into coils and loils of cowering dragon.

"I know," a hatchling squeaked like a row of freight cars braking. "That's the picture of Ethyl the Martyr and the Man in the Tin Suit."

"That's right, Marflagiggle. Very good. Now squat back down and I'll tell you the story."

We crept by. When we passed out of sight of the reptilian schoolroom we broke into a relieved, but hasty, trot. The last thing I heard as we ran into the distance, was "It was then that Ethyl realized that things were getting out of claw. She . . ."

After jogging for not quite as long as it seemed, we stopped for a while to breathe hard. "I guess I'll have to get married," I said when I had enough wind back to pretend I hadn't lost it. "With stories like this to tell," I explained to the puzzled stares, "it would be a shame not to have grandchildren to bore with them. 'Come sit on my knee, little girl, and Gramps will tell you about the time he audited a class of dragons.'"

"You desire little girl grandchildren?" Sylvia asked.

"The ones that sit on my knee had better be little girls," I explained.

Sylvia giggled. "All right, Gramps, I'll sit on your knee; but this time keep your hands to yourself."

"You learn fast," I told her. "Either that, or you have unplumbed depths."

"We carry different cultures," Sylvia said, brushing her long hair back from her face. "Sexual mores, for example . . . It might be fun for you to plumb my depths."

Chester, who was busy rubbing Dorothy's back and explaining about his fetish, suddenly stopped and peered off into the distance; a gesture that was becoming as common with us as with grouse, and for similar reason. "What," he complained, "now?"

A large dust cloud approached at a measured pace.

"Can you hear anything?" I asked Sylvia. "Hoofbeats?"

She shook her head. "Just some strange rumbling, grinding sound. It's been getting closer for the past few minutes."

"It must be coming from whatever's raising the dust then. Not horses. Cars or trucks?"

Now I heard it faintly in the distance. A steady, low rumbling that you seemed to hear as much with your feet as your ears. A sound associated with volcanoes and natural calamity. But not quite that. It was a noise that my body was familiar with, though my mind refused to identify. I closed my eyes and concentrated on the vibrations beneath my feet.

"A strange sound," Chester said. "One is tempted to say the gods are angry, but one will resist."

"Tanks!" I yelped.

"What for?"

"No, tanks. Big things with treads and guns. Named after generals."

"Ah," Chester said. "If they're ours they're named after generals. Hum. If it isn't one thing, it's an army."

I started to clamber up a tree to get a better look, but just then the dust cloud parted and the first monster rolled out.

"Must have come onto paved road," Chester commented.

"It won't be paved after they've gone over it," I said, stretching out on a low fork in the tree. "Those things rip hell out of even the best laid plans. I've seen them powder a new stressed-concrete highway. Each one of them weighs twenty-five or thirty tons."

"What kind are they?" Chester asked. "Or, at least, whose are they?"

I climbed up a few more notches and stuck my head out. "Oh, wow!"

"What? Wow, what?"

"They're Tigers. I saw one once at a base armory museum in Germany. The biggest and heaviest tanks ever made. Fifty tons. There won't be enough road surface left to ride a bicycle on. Hitler couldn't use them as much as he wanted because they ruined the roads for trucks and there wasn't anything big enough to transport them in. One of his secret weapons."

"Hitler?" Chester asked.

"Well, the *Wehrmacht*."

"What," Dorothy asked, "are you two talking about?"

"Later," Chester said. The rumbling and clanking was quite loud now, and the tanks were only a few hundred yards away. I could feel the tree I was in start to shake. "Those are Nazi tanks? I think we'd better get out of here."

"The war's been over since we were wee tads," I reminded him.

"Where you and I come from," Chester said. "Where the girls came from, it never happened. But here . . ."

"I get your point," I said, dropping out of the tree. "I think I saw a swastika on the turret of that monster in front. Let's split."

*"Halt!"* boomed a loudspeaker, blasting the air around us. *"You have been seen. Do not attempt to escape."* A sudden explosion cracked in my ears past the pain threshold and flame belched from the turret of the lead tank. Two seconds later a concussion blast rumpled the earth behind us in counterpoint as the shell landed, and a heat wave enveloped us and passed on. *"If you attempt to run you will be destroyed."*

"They've made their point," Chester said.

"What's happening?" Sylvia asked, a high edge of panic in her voice. "What are those things?"

"They're machines with men inside them," Dorothy said perceptively in a grim voice. "We can't get at them while they're in the machines, so we'll have to be nice until they get out." Single-minded woman. I agreed with her, reserving the hope that there'd be something we could do when they got out. Even these bloodthirsty girls would have little chance against machine guns. I decided that at the first chance, I'd better explain the function and capability of various hand weapons.

*"Throw down your arms."*

Chester called back, "We don't have any."

*"Resistance is futile. You will be well treated and placed in internment camps for the duration."*

The duration of what? I wondered. Us? The behemoths drew closer. For the first time, I regretted having been circumcised.

"If we scatter and run," Chester said, "they couldn't get all of us."

"I'd bet you on that if I thought I had any chance of collecting," I told him.

"Look!" Dorothy said. "Strangeness upon strangeness. What do they do?"

We looked. We stared. At the rear of the column of tanks, the dust cloud had been cloven in the air, as though cut with an axe, and half of it removed. To the left, the dust swirled and eddied as the tanks behind made finer particles of the chewed-up asphalt that the lead Tigers had converted the road into. To the right, nothing but clean air. As we watched, the vertical line of intersection, precise as a razor cut, moved steadily forward and left. "Godfrey!" I exclaimed brightly, "No dust."

"More," Chester said. "No tanks."

"No road!" Sylvia exclaimed.

I brought my eyes to ground level. Sure enough; where the razor edge passed it showed a different world: a fresh, unspoiled meadow, with a leaping brook and long, green grass. And the razor edge was approaching, shaving off tank after tank as it came.

"I think we're seeing a moving blip," Chester said. "The border between one probability world and another."

"It would be nice if we could get to that meadow world before those tank things get to us," Sylvia said, displaying a British capacity for understatement.

"There seem to be two levels, or maybe more," Chester said. "Light waves travel to and from the meadow world, but more material objects, like tanks, go somewhere else. It would be nice if our somewhere wasn't their somewhere, wherever it is." We were all huddled together and, somehow, holding hands.

*"Attention! Attention! You will immediately stop using your new secret weapon, or you will be destroyed completely. Immediately! I will count to five."*

"It isn't ours!" I yelled. "Honest it isn't."

*"One."*

Another tank blipped out but I could see that there'd be several left by five. I chose some curse words and aired them gently, stringing them together into strands of futile disgust.

*"Two."*

"Scatter and run like hell," Chester commanded urgently. "It's our only chance. I'm sorry girls, you picked a pair of errant knights. I hope, Michael, that your prayers are heard."

"I have no regrets," Sylvia said, squeezing our hands.

Dorothy grimaced. "If this is it, I regret not having a chance to find out what the dirk is happening."

*"Three."*

"Goodbye, Adolphus," Sylvia murmured. She pulled her hand free, and I realized how tightly I'd been holding it. "Goodbye, dear love," she whispered to me, and darted off toward the woods. I filed that away to think about later—if there was a later.

*"Ciao!"* Chester yelled, galloping away.

"See you around," I called, and was running.

Dorothy dropped to the ground and started squirming toward the lead tank.

BAROOM! Something kicked against the back of my head, and a large tree cracked to my left The earth dropped from under me and then rose up to hurt my knees. I ran several more steps before I realized that I was crawling. BAROOM! The earth came to meet me, and I tasted grass. A heavy chattering and roaring surrounded me. The scene had a quality of unreality, and I made a note to congratulate the theater manager on the excellence of his sound system. I hadn't heard heavy machine guns sound so real or so close since I qualified with fifties in the army. BAROOM! Something splatted against my face and shoulder. Why was I making those funny motions with my arms and legs? Oh, yes; I was running. But I was prone on the ground and my legs were kicking air. That would never do. I twisted around and climbed to my feet. Something soft and sticky ran down my face. BAROOM! A large hole opened to my right, and dirt sprayed out, stinging the side of my face like a thousand wasps and knocking me down. . . .

I sat For some time I sat, staring at a purple haze in front of me. Then I turned my head and stared at the purple haze to my left. I decided to lie down. Everything was quiet. I was deaf, I decided. Or dead. Or both.

[Are you all right?] Silly [Can you hear me?] Question. Silly question. [Oh, Michael!] Was someone out there? A vortex spread before me, beckoning and drawing me closer. At the bottom lay oblivion and the fall was eternal, and the thought was sweet.

Something stung the arm that was of my body. The vortex receded and I cried.

Something stung my arm, and my body again was me, and it hurt, and I screamed. And I woke.

"Michael, oh dear Michael, oh precious Bear," the litany went. I opened my eye and then my other eye and tried to focus.

Awareness flooded back to me. The pain receded, blocked off by what I recognized as chemical means. My face felt sticky all over, warm and sticky; but it was being wiped. Being wiped? I made an effort to focus past my nose and saw Sylvia's face above me, framed in a halo of pink light. "Angel," I said.

"What? I didn't understand, love. Say again."

I made an effort to coordinate. "Angel," I said. "Framed in a halo of light. But I think I'm alive."

"Yes. You were going into shock. It's lucky I'm a trained nurse and had my aidpack with me. Lie still for a minute."

"I didn't know you were a nurse. How long was I out? It felt like days, but it couldn't have been more than a few hours."

"I'm a nurse because it's my second job in the circus. Dorothy was too. You were unconscious for under a minute. I ran back to you the second that machine disappeared. The moving line hasn't reached us yet. About another," she squinted at the road, "thirty seconds." She wiped my eyes and the blood-halo disappeared. "I gave you a strong dead-pain dose so you can walk—I pray. We must move aside in case we go to the same world the Tiger machines did."

Sylvia planted her feet and pulled at my arm. I tried to gather my legs under me and push up. In a few seconds, I was on my feet and finding out how hard it is to balance when you have no sense of feeling. "Lean on me," Sylvia said, "we'll go faster."

"Don't be subtle," I said, swaying. "If I don't lean on you, we won't go at all. Did Chester and Dorothy make it?"

Sylvia looked at me for a long moment, considering. "I don't know the idiom," she said. "Look."

I looked. Across the clearing lay two bodies. One was—had been—Chester: clothing shredded, legs mashed and head twisted to an angle that life would not allow. The other body was unrecognizable. "Later," I said, "I shall be sick. Then I'll probably spend some time crying. I know it's happened, but I don't feel anything."

"You're crying," Sylvia said gently.

"I guess I am." I smiled weakly.

Something twisted my inside, whipped me around, and socked me in the solar plexus.

# BLIP

# 7

And, again, we were somewhere else. The first thing I did was to scout the area carefully and confirm my first impression—no tanks. The moving line sent them somewhere and us elsewhere. The second thing I did was collapse.

When I woke up I was between clean sheets over a soft mattress and Sylvia was sleeping in an upholstered chair beside the bed. The bed had posts sticking up from each of the four corners and a canopy overhead. The blue and yellow flowered pattern of the drapes around the bed was echoed by the smaller patterned curtains on the three small windows. The walls were covered with cleanly-scrubbed, but slightly peeling and faded print wallpaper. On the wall by the door was a framed photograph of a group of men in knickers standing by a camel, with the Sphinx and the Great Pyramid in the background. After gathering these impressions I lay back to think about them and to enjoy the sensation of breathing.

When I woke up again Sylvia was fussing with a tray. "Welcome back," she said. "Have some soup."

"How long," I asked after taking a sip of tomato soup, which was thoughtfully lukewarm, "have I been away?"

"Overnight," Sylvia told me, spooning some more soup into my mouth. She anticipated the next questions. "This house is about half a mile down the road from where you swooned. I walked until I reached it and told them you had been in an accident, and they came out to get you. They've been very nice, and I now have ridden in a car."

After I finished my bowl of soup, Sylvia took it downstairs and came back with Mrs. Siddens, the woman of the house. A matronly type in her fifties, dressed in calico except for a spotless white apron, she clucked over me and let me know that she'd be "consarned" if "them reckless fools in their motor cars aren't goin' to ruin the whole countryside; what with knocken' down fence posts, runnen' through barns, speeden' across the night at up to thirty miles an hour and honken' their horns at all hours, waken' a body up. And now they're goin' hitten' into people. They ought to be a law to regulate them machines, that's what Harry says!" She nodded her head emphatically up and down, while wringing her hands between the folds of her apron, creating a spreading wave of creases.

"You're a good woman, Mrs. Siddens," I told her. "And I thank you for what you've done for us. Harry, I take it, is your husband?"

"My man," she agreed. "He went into town this morn. Would have brought back a doctor, but your wife, bein' a trained nurse and all, said you wouldn't need one. You just lie there and take it easy; don't worry about a thing. It's our bound pleasure to help." Nodding forcefully several times, she retreated to the door and clumped downstairs.

"Hi, wife," I said to Sylvia, who had sat demurely through this.

"They assumed it when they picked you up," she explained. "They seemed to *want* to assume it, so I agreed."

"I agree also. Come to bed, wife."

Sylvia patted my head. "Mayhap sometime when you won't fall asleep. We'll see."

"Thanks," I said, leaning back weakly on the pillow. She was right: I fell asleep almost immediately.

When I woke up again I could tell I was better. I felt stronger and I was hungry. I swung my feet over the edge of the bed and stood up. A second later I was sitting down again. After a few minutes the dizziness had passed, and I was able to stay on my feet. My clothes were nowhere in sight, but a terrycloth robe had been hung behind the door. I put it on, wrapping it one and a half times around me, and belted it. The end dragged on the floor. Its owner, I deduced, was a large man. I giggled, pleased that I could deduce anything. Too much sleep must have made me slightly punch-drunk. Ah, well: the horrors of war. The thought that followed wasn't funny, and I suppressed it. I made my way gingerly down the stairs, heading toward a room from which I could hear the murmur of voices.

It was the kitchen, and the two girls were showing each other baking secrets and giggling over womanly things. They stopped talking as I walked in, and turned to stare at me. I felt as though I had accidentally penetrated to the ritual room of some mystic lodge and had almost overheard the most guarded arcane secrets.

> *For the land of Man is the whole of the world*
> *Which is his to fight and tame;*
> *But Woman by the kitchen fire*
> *Guards the eternal flame.*
> *And Man must quest for deeds and best*
> *The dark to renew his youth,*
> *While Woman, softly before the flame*
> *Speaks on the Ancient Truth.*

"Michael," Sylvia exclaimed. "Are you all right? How do you feel? Are you sure you should be out of bed?"

Mrs. Siddens nodded her head. "Just like a man. A full day he lies there, black to the world, weak as a kitten. Then he wakes up and *poof*, you can't keep him in bed twenty seconds so's he might get well on his own without suffrin' a relapse and haven' to get the doc in to take care of what nature would'f looked after pretty slick on her own iff'n a body would let her." Having given that speech, she smiled and all the wrinkles in her face fell into place so you could tell immediately how she'd gotten them. "Sit down and let's get some solid food into you, if you're bound determined to be out of bed."

I sat down and Sylvia came over and inspected me in her best nursery manner: checking my pulse, feeling my forehead with her lips, tapping and rubbing at me and peering into my left ear earnestly. I was afraid to ask her what she was looking for in my ear. "Will I pass?" I asked when she was through.

"Of the seventeen exercises we give as a test of physical condition, I doubt if you could pass one; but you'll live."

"Will I ever be able to play the piano?" I asked, unable to restrain the impulse.

"What's a piano?" Sylvia inquired.

"We have one in the parlor," Mrs. Siddens volunteered. "Do you play?"

"Only chopsticks and variations on a theme by chance."

"I *love* pianner music," she informed me, "and oprey and plays and mellerdrammer and the musicals the band puts on every summer on Sheepmeadow and the traveling Shakespeares and all them cultured things. I take Harry to all of 'em. He likes 'em too, but he ain't as enthusiastical as what I am."

"I'm sure," I told her. "It's wonderful to find someone who upholds the banner of culture." I was immediately ashamed of myself for having made fun of her and reassured to find that she hadn't noticed.

"All the wives around here are upholden' that there banner," she explained. "We takes our men to everythin' cultural what happens."

"That's wonderful," I said, staring earnestly into the bowl of oatmeal she had put in front of me and wondering what the long-suffering men felt about all this culture. The oatmeal had large islands of butter distributed throughout a lake of cream that almost overlapped the sides of the bowl. The lake bottom was white with sugar. A bit rich, I thought, for a sick man who doesn't nohow like oatmeal. Oh, well; mustn't offend mine hostess, who was certainly going out of her way to be kind and helpful to two strangers. I stirred the mess up until it attained the consistency of thick cement and spooned a gob into my mouth, trying to swallow without tasting it.

After the third gobfull, the taste snuck past my guard and banged into the gustatory reception centers. "Marf gloop!" I said, in some surprise.

"What did you say, husband?" Sylvia asked.

I swallowed. "That's good," I repeated. "Tacky, but good."

"Mind you eat it all before it hardens," Mrs. Siddens called from across the kitchen at the side table where she was chopping large yellow gourds into small yellow squares. "I got to go tend to my gardenin' now. You two make yourselves at home. If they's anythin' you want, don't ask." She gathered her apron about her and stalked out the kitchen door.

"Nice woman," Sylvia said. "I was helping her before you came down. Prester John but she can cook."

(Prester John?) "I'll bet it's a whole nice family," I said, determined to keep spooning the cereal into my mouth as long as I could. Already the mass in the bowl was tugging hard at the spoon each time I tried to lift it. "People don't grow in a vacuum, they affect each other. How can something this much like quick-setting cement taste so good?"

"I don't know," Sylvia admitted. "Have you ever tasted quick-setting cement?"

"You have a point."

"Her husband—her 'man'—Harry is also a kind and thoughtful soul. He's very big; that must be his bathrobe you're wearing. The youngest son is quiet and reserved; very polite. He's with his father. The eldest is away at school."

"You've learned a lot," I congratulated her. "Do you have any idea where we are?"

"In a province by name of Nebraska. It might also be of interest to know that the year in this, er, world is 1926 Anno Domini."

"It would seem that the time rates are different in the various worlds," I said. "Judging by what I see around me, this could be the 1926 from the history of my world. I wish Chester were here."

"Now . . ."

"It's all right," I assured her. "Just a random thought. We'll stick to the main cause, and no crying for the dead until after the battle."

"Are we in a battle?" Sylvia asked.

"It may not have started yet," I told her, "but the lines are drawn and the skirmishers are out. That long sleep seems to have given my subconscious a chance to work, and I have a vague notion of what's happening, although not why or how. But I intend to find out."

"Tell me," Sylvia said, perching on the side of the table.

I found that while I had been speaking the spoon had taken root in the oatmeal, sticking straight up; and I couldn't budge it. I picked up spoon, oatmeal and bowl like a large candy apple and waved it about to punctuate my explanation. "The blips," I said, "are new and widespread. The last we were in must have been some sort of focus or node, since that mix of people was too varied to have come from the same culture, or cultural mix. My guess is that they are in some way artificial and caused by the people, or things, in the saucers."

"Why?"

"Because the saucers seem to be around when they happen, and seem very interested in the results. Maybe we're part of a vast scientific experiment on the part of a people who have learned to manipulate space-time, whatever that is. All I know is where I come from scientists talk about it as though it exists, and if it exists someone will find a way to use it."

"We have an apparatus that does something like that," Sylvia told me.

"Like what?" I asked.

"I don't understand it at all. Maybe the arithmeticking is beyond all I was taught, but I have been on craft that made use of it."

"In what way?" I demanded. "Skipping through worlds? Why didn't you mention it before?"

"Not world skipping in this sense, but the other. When the Arcturians discovered us they invited us to join the Federated Cloud and gave us the knowledge to build the mechanism that made star travel possible. It does something that I don't understand to the space-time rate of change around the stellar craft while they travel. But it just feels like a slight bump, nothing at all like that horrible wrench that does these things."

I said, "They might be related. Say, you mean you've been to different planets? You've traveled on these interstellar, er, craft?"

"Yes, since I was a small girl. The Great World Circus and Barnum Show goes on tour for four to six months every year or so. That is, we spend a year here and then four to six months traveling. I've been on tour four, no five, times. I've seen many different worlds and slept under many different suns. That's a circus joke, because we usually sleep during the day."

"Do you know that my ambition has always been to make it to the Moon or Mars before I die? And you've traveled to many different . . ."

"The Moon is dead, just a transfer point. I was there twice. Good hotels. I've never been to Mars, but I understand it's quite beautiful in season."

"Shut," I declared passionately, "up!"

"Why, Michael, what's the matter?"

"Never mind. I'm sorry. You wouldn't understand." I sighed. "Never been in a car, but she's been between the stars."

"The trains take us anywhere we want on Earth. They're very fast and dependable. If I remember from history we tried personal mechanical vehicles for a short time, but gave them up as a bad idea. They smell up the road, take up too much room, caused many accidents and just proved a general nuisance. They were outlawed forty or fifty years ago. I've seen them in museums, but they didn't look anything like the ones on your world. More like the ones here."

"I agree," I told her. "They're dirty, smelly, dangerous and all that. Maybe we should have had the benign influence of Arcturians on our world."

"Oh, we gave them up before we were broached."

"What are the cars like here?"

"Oh, you'll see when Mrs. Siddens' man Harry comes back. What are we going to do now?"

"I guess I didn't make that clear," I said. "We're going to go on and search for the source of these happenings. It's liable to be dangerous, but staying here might be just as dangerous, so we fight. Wait a minute, maybe I shouldn't have said 'we' so quickly. It *is* going to be dangerous if I manage to get close to the heart of this mess, so it might be better if you wait here or let me settle you some place safe until this is over."

"Michael!"

"I'll come back for you, you know that."

"That isn't nearly the point. First of all, if you go blip and I don't, you may not be able to come back. Second of all, what makes you think I'd let you go alone? You'll need me. And I need you, even if I have to walk through the Valley of Dread to be at your side. Third of all, I have to find Adolphus, and you swore to help me. I will grant that the new quest must be striven first, but after, we have a unicorn to find."

"A curious mixture, you," I said, pulling her firmly toward me over the bowl of cement and commencing a lengthy kiss of agreement, exploration, adoration and lust.

"Ahum, hem, hem," coughed the doorway, and we unwillingly separated and looked up. Mrs. Siddens stood there, turnips in hand, flanked by the tallest, widest, most genial looking giant I've ever seen in human form.

The giant gave a happy roar. "Must be feelin' a mite better," he declared. "Sure looks better than when we carted him in here."

"My man Harry," Mrs. Siddens introduced. She reached behind him and pulled a smaller version into view. "This here's my youngest, Tanner."

I stood up and extended my hand. "It's a pleasure to meet both of you. I have a lot to thank you for."

Harry waved his gigantic mitt. "Nothin'," he said, sounding embarrassed. "We do what we can for each other and try to live by His words, and I guess that's what makes us human."

"I think, maybe, you've got a point there," I agreed. "We thank you anyway."

"Yes," Sylvia added. "We do so thank you for your kindness. We were fortunate indeed to have come upon our trouble so close to one who practices his belief, good sir."

"Shucks," Harry boomed. "Say, if you don't mind my askin', where do you haul from?" He immediately managed to look sorry he'd asked such a personal question.

Sylvia looked puzzled for a second, then correctly figured the idiom out. "I'm from Boston," she told him.

"That makes it right," Harry said. "I reckoned as you weren't from around here by the way you talk. Not," he added quickly, "that you sound funny or anythin', just different."

They insisted about then that I go upstairs and rest, and I didn't put up much of an argument except to assert that we'd stay one more night, thank you very much, then stop imposing on their hospitality. Harry reckoned as how we'd see about that.

Sylvia came upstairs later with a dinner tray and I repeated the same thing to her between mouthfuls, throwing in words like "mission" and "duty" and the like. She agreed that we should leave as soon as possible, but said it would be silly if I was too weak to do anything but collapse further on. She made it sound like a cavalry officer assessing the strength of his mount. No emotional appeals from this girl. I went to sleep feeling the need to be cuddled and reassured and bravely not mentioning it to anyone. It was sometime later before I realized that Sylvia probably could also have used some reassurance about then.

The next morning I felt as strong as a lion. A sick lion. But I was resolved that today we would continue our quest. "Today," I told Sylvia when she came in, "we split. Where are my clothes?"

"Split," she said. "I like that." She went off to fetch my wardrobe. It had, I found when she returned, been all neatly washed, patched and pressed. Just the way I like it: no starch. I dressed, trying not to wince at the sore spots, and came downstairs.

Over a hearty breakfast of quick-setting cement, pancakes, eggs, ham and coffee, I told our host and hostess that I was fine, that we had to continue our way east today, and that I didn't know how to repay them for their kindness. The last was literally true, as I was sure that I didn't have anything that would pass for cash in this world.

Our host was glad I was so much better, happened to be going to town early afternoon, where we could get a train, and wouldn't think of accepting anything for his help. I got around this moral dilemma by making him accept a ring I'd been wearing for the past ten years. It was very fine silver, worked intricately into the shape of two dragons grinning at each other. I picked it up during an occult phase I had wandered through. He admired it and, since the representation was rather obscure, I left it to him to decide what two creatures were accomplishing what ends.

The car which we settled in back of, Harry and his son rather thoroughly taking up the front, was an honest-to-gosh Model T. They started it up and we drove out on to the road, waving our frantic goodbyes to Mrs. Siddens, who stood by the kitchen door wringing her apron.

Many rattles, gasps, wheezes and bumps later, a town appeared ahead of us; sticking up through the flat land like a child's play village on a table top. We passed a series of signs that welcomed the Lions, Elks, Moose, Rotarians and other animals to Ogallala, Nebraska, and told us where the Baptist, Reform, Congregational, Methodist, Catholic and Non-Denominational churches were. Five minutes later we were noisily proceeding down the main street of Ogallala, Nebraska, and being chased or stared at by an assortment of small dogs, large cats, dirty children and several less identifiable objects.

The car rattled, gasped and wheezed to a stop in front of a long-unpainted building with two shiny new tin signs tacked to the front. One said SPUD and the other MOXIE. "This here's where I'm goin'," Harry declared. "Station's down t'other end of the street."

We thanked him again and headed down t'other end of the street.

"Where are we going?" Sylvia asked me. I admired her for not bringing it up before.

"I don't know," I told her. "Except east. The blips seem to be moving east, and taking us a bit further that way each time, so we'll either keep up with them or head them off. I want to get a closer look at one of those flying saucers. Beyond that, I have no plan."

"May I, perchance, mention two small concerns?" Sylvia asked so quietly that I knew I had overlooked something important.

"What?" I asked, assuming my Fount of all Knowledge guise.

"The first is that I'd just as soon not be on a rapidly-moving vehicle when we go through another blip."

"You're right," I agreed. "Although you can't really call these trains, if I remember correctly, rapidly moving vehicles."

"The second," she continued, "is: how are we going to pay for a ticket?"

I honestly hadn't thought of that. "I'll think of something," I assured her.

We went into the station and confronted the dour-looking man with a peaked hat several sizes too small for him who resided behind the barred window. "When is the next train east?" I inquired.

"Tomorrow," he divulged. "About noon."

"Oh," I said intelligently. "Then we've missed today's train?" Harry had said that he thought it left late afternoon.

"Nope," Dour-Puss informed us, tilting the cap back to a rakish angle over his ears, "leaves tomorrow, 'bout noon. Tomorrow's train leaves 'bout six, if it comes in."

"Thank you," I said. "Could you recommend a hotel in town?"

"Nope."

"Thanks again. See you tomorrow."

"Yup," he said sorrowfully.

"Well," Sylvia said, as we walked back up the hot pavement. "What do we do now?"

"I'll think of something."

"You said that."

I glared at her. She glared back at me. I sighed. "I think our tempers could use a cool drink," I suggested. "Let us find a place to sit down."

"And use what for money?"

"I knew it," I said. "Our first fight, and it's about money."

We trudged on for a while, then came face to face with a sign that swung gently in the slight breeze.

### OGALLALA MANSIONS
TRANSIENT—PERMANENT
*Rooms—$1.00 up.    In Advance*

Sylvia stopped and stared wistfully at it. I stopped. "Well, we could always rob a bank."

"Humor!" Sylvia snorted, and we walked on.

Sylvia grabbed my arm. "Look," she said, pointing down a side street. I looked, ready for anything from a tank to a moving blip. What I saw was a collection of tents, two large surrounded by numerous small. "A circus," Sylvia exclaimed happily.

"Are you sure?"

"Of course. Nothing looks like a circus but a circus." She was, I realized, right. One, or even two large tents could have been anything from a revival meeting to a National Guard outing, but that collection could have been nothing but a circus or carnival. Particularly, now that I got a good look, with that erratic swashing of primary colors over everything. This was the one thing that looked pretty much the same throughout most of recorded history. The attractions it offered didn't vary much either.

"Should we go?" I asked, thinking that a walk around the grounds might cheer both of us up.

"Of course," she said. "Circus people always help each other. It's an ancient tradition." By Godfrey, she *was* from a circus. This wasn't just a show to cheer her up, this was the closest thing to home she could find on this world. We headed to the main gate.

A bored man in an American flag striped suit stood behind the raised ticket stand. "Ten cents admission," he said in an impossibly animated voice. "The greatest show on Earth. Toured before the crown heads of Europe. Two rings, in which you will see performed the feats of skill and daring which have amazed and astonished the most hardened, the most cynical, the most blasé audiences from New York to the New Hebrides. Only ten cents, one thin dime, one-tenth part of a dollar for admission to the midway, where you can see, before the main show starts, some of the most startling, enlightening, educational personalities that have ever graced the concert stages of the world. Melton's world-famous menagerie, where the wild beasts of the forest and jungle are kept in their native habitats. Dr. Samuel Johnson's educational freak show, where unbelievable oddities, both bestial and human, are exhibited while the doctor discourses on the wonders of God's world in the lecture he has been called upon to deliver before learned men of science both here and abroad. See Malik, the India-rubber man; Georgiana, half man, half woman; the Wild Man of Borneo, who will devour a live chicken before your very eyes. The main show starts in ten minutes. Only ten cents, one thin dime, one-tenth part of a dollar. . . ."

Sylvia shouldered her way through the small crowd at the gate, towing me in her wake. "Palley!" she said in an urgent whisper. "I'd like a glim at the strawboss. We're looking for a grift."

The barker leaned forward. "What's your hustle?" he asked, in a normal voice.

Sylvia shrugged. "I work with animals," she said. "But we'll take about anything: shill, runner, wipe-out, any grift short of geeking for a little bread."

"A little bread is all you'll get from this tinplate outfit," he said, nodding us through. "The wheel's behind the main tent. If he's not there, ask." He straightened up. "The greatest show on Earth. Only ten cents . . ."

We hurried down the midway, past signs with too many coats of gaily-colored paint, platforms with almost-scantily clad girls and an incredible din of competing attractions. Suddenly something caught my eye and I stopped. On a platform in front of a small tent a tall, thin man in the robes of a mystic, with the erratically-trimmed ends of thinning, blonde hair sticking out from under his turban, was discoursing to a small, but interested crowd. I stepped closer.

"Come along," Sylvia said, with the annoyed air of a mother whose son has stopped to look in a candy store window when she's in a hurry. "You can look at the acts later; we have to see the strawboss."

"Wait a minute," I said. "Just be quiet and have faith; I think the improbable is happening again." We approached the man, who was declaiming a set speech in a trained, powerful voice:

"Throughout the ages, Man has always tried to peer beyond the veil that separates him from eternity. Some have used the crystal to help clear away the mists; to sharpen their vision. What is it that makes this possible? Could it be some unknown, undiscovered property of the crystal glass that penetrates the fog, or does the crystal merely serve as a focus for the inner concentration of the mystic? It doesn't matter; what is important is that some people have been gifted with the ability—with the crystal's aid— to peer into the future and to survey the past. To such people both future and past lie as an open book, to be read at will and to provide the answers to those perplexing questions that trouble us all.

"For the small sum of ten cents, to be paid to my lovely assistant here, I will endeavor to take a small group—no more than seven at a time—on a trip into the innermost reaches of the mind itself, and lay bare the secrets of past and future. For those who desire a more complete reading, private sessions are available at a small additional fee, and can be arranged on request.

"Thank you for your patience, my friends. And now I must enter the inner chamber to have a moment for meditation and prepare myself for our trip into the unknown depths of the human mind, into the innermost reaches of the crystal; which is an ancient glass, sacred to the goddess Sekmet, which I received as a reward, a gift, for my services over many years to the Department of Egyptian Antiquities of the British Museum. A token of their esteem for the small aid I was able to render them, because of my many years of study of the great, lost secrets of the past, in deciphering and unraveling the mysteries of that ancient civilization which passed with all its glories and feats as yet unduplicated by our modern science, many centuries before the dawn of the Christian Era.

"My assistant will take your money." With a last grand gesture, he disappeared behind the folds of the tent.

"Very impressive," Sylvia admitted. "Can we go now?"

"Come with me," I said, pulling her toward the tent. The crowd was breaking up now, but a good number of them had stayed to form a sort of ragged line to the left of the tent, where a pretty brunette in circus tights was exchanging dimes for tickets.

"Don't tell me," Sylvia said. "Perchance are you going to ask the seer, Professor," she read the small sign, "Waters for a glimpse into the future to advise us?"

"You're not so far off at that," I said, pulling a disgusted Sylvia to the front of the line.

"Twenty cents, please," the brunette said, smiling sweetly and holding two tickets out to us.

"Would you please deliver a message to the professor?" I asked, putting on my most winning smile. "It's very important, and he'll be glad to get it, you have my word."

Her smile disappeared. "Right now?"

"Yes, please."

"Well, okay. I've sold about three groups ahead anyway." She stood up, gathering tickets and money box about her. "Would the first seven please enter the tent? I'll be right back out to sell tickets to the rest of you, please be patient. Thank you." She got halfway to the tent door before she stopped and turned around. "Say, what's the message?"

"Tell him," I told her carefully, "to watch out for the revolving door."

"The what? Say, is this a gag?"

I assured her that it wasn't. I had to assure her several times before she turned and went into the tent.

"All right," Sylvia said. "To me you can explain it. Is that another one of your idioms?"

"You should talk after that exchange with the guy at the gate," I told her. "No, it's a private joke between Tom and me."

"Tom?"

"Unless I'm going blind as well as deaf," I explained, "the good professor is none other than my old friend Tom Waters. He disappeared about two weeks ago, and this might explain why—or, at least, where."

"I see," Sylvia said. "He took an earlier blip."

"Hrmph!" I said.

"But, about this revolving door . . ."

Brunette came out, swinging her hips in a much more friendly manner. "The professor will see you," she said in a low, suggestive voice. Now I *was* someone. Sylvia glared. "Go back around the tent," Brunette said, "there's an entrance."

We clambered over the platform and rounded the tent. Tom, minus his turban, was standing by the flap. In an extreme display of joyous delight at seeing each other again, we shook hands. "That's no revolving door," Tom informed me, continuing the old vaudeville riff we'd used as a catchphrase lo these many years, "that's my mother!"

"Your mother?" I questioned, unbelievingly. "What's her name?"

"Sam."

"Sam? That's funny, that's my name!"

Tom opened his arms wide. "Mother!"

"Son!" We pantomimed an embrace.

We both faced out toward an imaginary audience and broke into a softshoe routine. "We are the joyboys of radio," we sang/hollered in unison, "so let's go, let's go, let's go!"

Tom bent over and marched solemnly in place. "Trudging through the muck and mire . . ."

"Hello, Muck," I interrupted, extending my hand.

"Hello, Mire!" Tom took the hand and we gave a quick, stiff-arm, double up-and-down.

I did a breakaway fast shuffle and started a two-step. "Hello, Joe; what do you know?"

Tom faded his palms in and out, in the ancient Eddie Cantor gesture. "Just got back from the animal show!"

"Rah-di-dah, rah-di-dah . . ." and we both did a slow shuffle off our imaginary stage.

Sylvia was standing ten feet away with her mouth open. It was the first time I'd seen her entirely nonplussed. "What," she was finally able to gasp out between the combined tears of laughter and rage that our routine usually provoked in the unwary, "do you call that?"

"That," Tom informed her, drawing his usual somber pose back around himself like a mantle, "was a demonstration of what killed vaudeville. We've always had a soft spot for funerals." He turned and looked me over very carefully. "It *is* you. Anyway, it has to be you; no one else could possibly know that routine or have the brainless abandon to do it. How did you manage to get thrown into the past too?"

"That's not exactly where it's at," I told him. "It'll take a while to explain. Any place where we can sit down over a cup of coffee?"

"You know my famous habits," Tom said. "Soft drinks, only soft drinks. I'm developing a taste for Moxie. Don't introduce me to the lovely young lady; I'm not sensitive."

"Tom," I said, "Sylvia. Sylvia, Tom. You won't like each other."

"When you cop other people's lines," Tom said severely, "at least give credit." He kissed Sylvia's hand. "Lovely child," he said. "I must leave you to earn some filthy lucre, but I shall be with you in but a brief time. Take heart! You can wait for me over there in the cook tent. Tell Fran to give you a couple of mugs of coffee. Who knows; she might even spring for a few doughnuts. I'll be with you as soon as I tell a few of the marks that there's oil on the land, love in the air, profit in taking that big step, and life in the old girl yet. Whatahell, whatahell. What a racket. Be with you faster than you could possibly believe." Tom disappeared behind the flap, and we headed over to the cook tent. Sylvia seemed slightly stunned.

After I had seated her at a long, wooden table and brought over two mugs of coffee from an incredibly ancient urn and its incredibly fat watchwoman, she came out of her trance. "I like him," she said.

"That's nice," I said. "Try not to overdo it. You wouldn't want to see two old friends fighting over a woman, would you?"

"Don't be silly," she said. "Not like that! I just like him."

"Ha!"

"I think he's good for you," Sylvia explained. "And anything that's good for you, I like."

Hmm. I drank my coffee, slightly reassured.

Tom appeared after a while, devoid of his Mandrake suit, and sat across from us with a large bottle of soda. "I've taken an hour break," he announced. "Got a few private readings lined up then. A lot more bread in the private readings: up to two bucks a throw."

"Is that why you don't announce a price outside?" I asked.

"Sure," he said. "I size them up when they come in: suit, haircut, jewelry, mannerisms; I can peg down to a penny what they'll spring for. Sherlock Holmes would be proud of me."

"Ah!" I said, shaking my head. "The world lost a great private detective when you became a performer, Mr. Waters."

Tom pressed a finger alongside his hawk-shaped nose. "Ah, Watson," said he, "I commend to your attention what the dog did in the nighttime."

"But Holmes," I protested, "the dog did nothing in the nighttime."

"You are mistaken, Watson," my old friend declared, "and if you would examine your shoe, I believe you will find traces of it there."

I examined my shoe. "Astounding, Holmes," I said.

"Elementary, my dear Watson," he replied.

Sylvia was staring from one to the other of us like a referee watching a hot ping-pong match. "You're going to drive me crazy," she announced. "Is that, perchance, another of your vaudeville thingies?"

Tom looked at her in amazement. "You've never heard of Sherlock Holmes?" he asked.

"She's not illiterate," I assured him. "I'll explain."

"Do," Tom demanded. "And, along with that, explain what you said before about this not exactly being the past. Here I thought I was giving the robes a clear steer into the future because I honest-to-God knew it."

"I promise," I said. "But you first. I have a feeling yours is simpler."

"All right," Tom agreed. He took a deep swig of soda. "It all started the last night I saw you. That is, I saw you that afternoon, and then came the last night. You know what I mean?"

"Yes," I said

"Good. I don't, not anymore. Anyway, a friend of mine, Dr. Dee by name, had just perfected a new version of the Girl in the Trunk illusion; you know the one?"

"I do. It was Houdini's favorite for many years, except with him it was a man in the trunk."

"That's it. It can be used either as a great illusion or a great escape. This time it was again to be the man in the trunk. No escape, just illusion. The difference," he explained to Sylvia, "is in the presentation. If a girl enters the trunk, is sealed in, then the magician waves his magic thing around several times and the trunk is revealed empty, with the girl standing outside and every lock and seal intact, including the ones with the spectator's initials, it is an illusion since the magician is thought to have worked the magic from outside the trunk. If the magician, heavily manacled, is placed inside the trunk, which is then sealed as above, and after several heart-stopping minutes (because there is only a limited amount of air to breathe inside the sealed trunk) he appears outside the still-sealed trunk and the manacles, still closed, are found inside; it's an escape. A great escape. It's all in the presentation.

"Anyhow, as I said, it was to be the Man in a Trunk. Me. Dr. Dee has gained a bit of weight over the years, and he found that he couldn't fit inside the trunk any more; and it's hard to escape from a trunk unless you first get into it. So he asked me to assist him. Having nothing on for the evening, and happening to have the traditional tuxedo freshly back from the cleaners, I agreed.

"It was, I remember, about ten o'clock when Dr. Dee called me on stage and introduced me to the substantial audience. Professor Waters, he declared, the world's foremost escape artist, just back from a triumphant tour of the finest prisons in the world. I bowed to the audience and explained a little about the history of escapes, the glorious tradition that demonstrates to every man that stone walls do not a prison make, and that the greatest obstacles can be overcome with a little knowledge and the strength and persistence of man's great will to survive. I didn't mention, of course, that a few lockpicks carefully secreted about the person might be of more help.

"A select committee of volunteers was called up from the audience, with nary a stooge among the lot. They examined me and the trunk with the most minute care, noticing everything but what mattered. Satisfied that in their collective wisdom—one was a doctor, one a lawyer and one the sheriff of the county; all very carefully trained to observe—that they had missed nothing, they manacled me with handcuffs and leg irons that the sheriff, who had probably never seen a leg iron until that second, pronounced legitimate and secure. I hobbled over to the trunk and stepped inside, informing the audience at this point that Dr. Dee would stand by with an axe to chop me out quickly if anything went wrong, as there was only enough air in the closed trunk to support life for between four and five minutes. Then I sat down in the trunk and doubled over so the lid could be closed."

Tom stared moodily into the little hole on top of the soda bottle. "Then came the first problem. While I could still hear the committee outside fastening the seals, I set to work on the manacles. The first three, the leg irons, presented no problem, and I was out of them in less time than it took to fasten them around my legs."

"Oh," Sylvia said, fascinated. "How did you do it?"

Tom fixed her with a steady look. "Years of practice and self-denial," he told her earnestly, "and eating yak dung in the Orient. The yak dung, I think, was the deciding factor."

Sylvia shrugged elaborately. "Magicians!" she said, from the bottom of her circus soul. "I should have known. Aerialists, animal acts, jugglers, clowns; everyone else in carney is delighted if you're interested in their grift. Magicians won't even let you unload their props. You'd think what they did was magic, or something."

I laughed. Tom looked at Sylvia with something approaching respect "Where did you pick her up?" he demanded.

"Later," I said. "Finish the yarn."

"Righto, mate. Where was I? Oh, the yak dung, yes. The leg irons were off before the committee had retreated to behind the screen which now, I assume, shielded the trunk from the audience. The first handcuff wouldn't yield to the most, er, elaborate persuasion. Gently cursing Dee and berating myself for not having taken the elementary precaution of checking the things before the show, I went to work on the other three. Two of them slid smoothly open like a safe door under the fingers of Willie the Actor Sutton."

"I think Sutton just robbed banks," I said, "I don't think he cracked safes."

Tom favored me with a withering glance. "Similes and legends," he informed me loftily, "take on a life of their own. Now: the two remaining handcuffs, both bright and shiny so they probably weren't rusted closed or sprung-jammed . . ."

"How could you tell in the dark?" Sylvia asked.

"I shine with the radiant light of the good at heart. As I say, these two cuffs wouldn't open for love or money. I started sweating. I could have worked the gimmick and left the trunk with the cuffs on my wrist, but my professional pride prevented me from doing that. It would be better to let Dr. Dee swing that axe and cut me out half-asphyxiated than to come out half-escaped. But I didn't want to ruin Dee's trunk. Besides, there was a good question as to whether that ancient fire-axe could make a dent in the iron body of the trunk. If it did, he'd probably bash it into the side of my head, which wasn't too many fractions of an inch away from the trunk wall. By now four minutes had passed."

"Was the air starting to get bad?" Sylvia asked.

"No," Tom told her. "I was using an ancient Yoga system of breathing which would enable that feeble air supply to last me for an indefinite length of time. I struggled on with the cuffs, wasting about half a minute getting angry and yanking them from side to side until I had thoroughly bruised my wrists. Then cool reason prevailed. I returned to gentle, scientific techniques; and in a moment discovered my mistake with one of the cuffs. In another moment it was off, and I attacked the remaining one with renewed vigor. Suddenly there was an earth-shaking jolt. For a minute I thought Dee was attacking the trunk with his axe. Then I realized that it would take a dozen men with axes to make that much din and vibration. I decided that's what it was—twelve men with fire-axes attacking my poor trunk. I drew myself into a corner as much as I could, which was damn little, and waited for the first chop to go through my leg.

"Then it was over. All was silent. And my trunk was upright where before it had been flat on the floor. Wondering exactly what had happened, I let my subconscious work on the cuff. My subconscious, always better at these things than I am, had it off in a few seconds. I reached around for the cleverly-disguised lever that activated the gimmick.

"It wasn't there!

"I felt around the area where it should be, and my questing fingers encountered plush; nice, soft plush, where but moments before the hardwood inside of the Dee escape trunk had been.

"The next few minutes, I confess, are a haze. I didn't flip out or panic or anything like that. I just went into a small, red haze. When I came out of it my subconscious again came through for me. Without thinking, I prodded in a certain direction and twisted in another. The side of the trunk swung open like the top of Dracula's coffin, and I stumbled out on to the hardwood floor. I realized what had happened as I left the trunk: my fingers, unbidden, had pressed the sequence for releasing the Houdini trunk escape, and mind you I haven't so much as seen a Houdini trunk (which was not the one used by Houdini, but a trade name adopted for a much older one by the new manufacturer after Houdini was where he couldn't argue) in fifteen years.

"Then I realized something else. The hardwood floor I had stepped out on to was not the highly-polished floor of the theater stage, but an unfinished-wood slat platform. To be exact, it was the baggage platform of the train station in Ogallala, Nebraska.

"My first thought was a vast practical joke. I had been drugged and taken out here, at great expense, to amuse my friends. Then, after closing the trunk and entering the station, I learned that it was something else. I, Tom Waters, had traveled through time over fifty years," He took a few deep breaths and finished the soda. "That's my story."

"How'd you get here?" I asked.

"You mean the carney?" Tom smiled. "What else could I do? I didn't have a dime, I was dressed in a fancy tuxedo, and I was thrust deep into the past. I needed someplace where I could sort of disappear for a while and sort things out; to try to find out what had happened and what I could do about it Also, I needed bread. The only place where I could find both bread and invisibility was a carney, where nobody asks questions and where I had a marketable skill. If worse came to worse I could always pitch the old ace in the hole."

"The old what?" I asked. I had never realized how deep in the lore of both magic and carnivals Tom had immersed himself.

"The ace in the hole of every professional mystic is peddling fortunes, usually astrological. William Lindsay Gresham, author of *Nightmare Alley,* one of the finest books ever written about carney, put it this way—or will put it this way, this time business has me confused:

> *Some ladle out the blarney*
> *In the mitt camp of a carney*
> *And some lecture on the Cosmic Oversoul*
> *But their names would be mud*
> *Like a chump playing stud*
> *If they lost that old ace in the hole."*

"That's very pretty," Sylvia said.

"I thank you," Tom said, "and Bill Gresham thanks you. Now, let's hear it. How'd you get here?"

"You'd better get another soda, or maybe two," I warned him. He took me at my word and went off for two more bottles. Sylvia replenished our mugs of hot mud, and we settled back down.

"It started about a week ago," I told Tom. "Time gets a little confused around here, but anyway it's about two weeks after you disappeared." I went on to relate just what happened to us since Sylvia misplaced her unicorn. I drew as detailed a picture as I could pluck out of my memory, since I wanted Tom to have every clue, every scrap of information, to see if he could come up with any additions or changes to my basic conclusions.

# 8

"Hmm," Tom said some time later. "Yes. Well. So Chester's gone off to meet the, ah, final conductor. I'm sorry to hear that. Done in by a tank. He would much rather have died in bed, or even in Philadelphia. Unicorn, huh?" He took a final swig on the latest bottle of soda. "Flying saucers. That's something to think about. And I think I can give you something to think about." He pulled away from the table. "I have some, ahem, clients to see now: private readings. I'll be back in about an hour and a half."

"What are you going to give us to think about?" I asked.

"I'll tell you when I get back. Think about it while I'm gone."

He left and we thought about it. While we were thinking, the cook tent started to fill up: muscular men and women in brightly-spangled costumes who walked on the balls of their feet; ape-like weight lifters in tights; clowns; midgets; ballerinas; hard-faced men in riding dress who walked with short whips clenched under their arms like British colonels; roustabouts and ringmasters: the kaleidoscopic variety of people that make up the normal circus world perched themselves on tables and benches all around us, and loud and happy conversation filled the air. Sylvia smiled and relaxed, she was at home. I couldn't understand a word of it.

*"So this frail miffed on the catchout, see, and I was left gawkers . . ."*

*"When Rueben brought the arm and papered us and we had to take it on the uppers . . ."*

*"I'm taking my stint on the box when I glom this makeup keeping it cozy. Firstoff I think she's shilling, but the man says I'm colddecking it, so I figure it must be my swells . . ."*

"You understand any of this?" I asked Sylvia. "I feel like it's my first day in French class."

Sylvia gave a wide shrug that encompassed the universe. "The same as any other group," she told me. "They're either talking about work or women."

"Oh." We drank some more coffee and joined into a few of the conversations when people sat at our table. They quickly lost interest when they found we weren't with the circus and they had never heard of the circus Sylvia had been with (surprise, surprise!), but they were all friendly and jovial. Fran, the fat lady and today's cook-tent minder, was going from table to table plunking down large bowls from a gigantic tray. When she reached our table, two of the bowls were plunked in front of us. Meatballs and spaghetti filled them almost to the overflow point, and they smelled delicious.

"Thank you very much," I said, looking down regretfully, "but we can't . . ."

"Shut up," Fran announced. "Eat!"

We did. Somehow, during the course of the meal someone managed to sneak mugs of red wine by our plates. Knowing better than to argue, we finished these without protest. Half an hour later we were relaxed, happy and full.

A man with a bushy moustache and an air of command sat down opposite us. He was reading a letter and making occasional mumbles of indignant outrage. "I ask you," he suddenly shouted, waving the letter to my left. "I ask you, what am I supposed to do with this?"

I looked to my left and discovered that Tom had quietly seated himself and was munching a peanut butter sandwich. "With what?" he asked.

"Thissere letter. What are they telling me? Who do they think I am?" He thrust the letter at Tom, who took it and began reading. The man transferred his attention to me. "I wrote asking what happened to my subscription, see? Like I subscribed month ago, and I never got more than one issue. So they sent me this letter."

Tom passed me the letter. Under the heading *CRAW-DADDY! the magazine of grok.,* was the following text:

Dear Mister Throck,

We are sorry to inform you that our frog is sick. We used your subscription money for cigars (we've been really short on cigars around here), and now the frog. It's difficult to express our sense of regret in one letter, what with the frog lying fallow in the Bide-a-Wee. We toss sleeplessly each night, not knowing if his merry croak will ever sound again or if he will go off to that great lilypad in the sky; and then there's the matter of the cigars, which it turns out the frog has been munching on for sometime.

Until we can get more money from gentle people like yourself, it seems unlikely that anything can be done, as both the veterinary and the tobacconist have rather callously cut off our credit. We are presently advertising like mad for new subscribers, and as the local papers don't know as yet of our plight, we expect to be able to continue this ruse for several weeks, by which time we hope to have the frog back and the tobacconist's friendship intact.

Thank you for your courteous inquiry. We hope this answers all your questions.

Sincerely,
*Carol Hunter*
Explanation Editor

P. S. We have just been informed that the frog was unable to digest the cigars and is now comatose. An X-ray (at remarkably high cost) reveals that he swallowed them whole and, since the amphibian digestive system seems unable to cope with tobacco, he is not expected to live.

The problem now is whether to cut him open and retrieve the cigars, or merely light one end and pass him among a few intimate friends. You realize how serious this could become.

We'll get back to you soon.

"I'm sorry, Throck," Tom said. "I have no idea of what to advise. These people seem to have a mind of their own."

"Yeah," Throck said, snatching the letter back from me and stuffing it into a pocket, "and I'll bet they keep it in a little glass jar. They sound like a bunch of perverts." He got up and stomped off.

"Well," Tom said, hunching across the table like a large hawk, "the question is, what now?"

"What did you have to tell us before you left?" I asked.

"Oh, yes. Two things. First: I've seen one of the flying saucers."

"When?"

"A couple of days ago. No, as a matter of fact, it was three days ago. It was early evening and the thing came and hovered over the grounds for a few minutes and then took off like a bat out of Mammoth Cave."

"What did it do?" Sylvia asked.

"Nothing. It didn't pull a people-eating act like the one you describe. It didn't even alarm the rubes. Most of them thought it was one of them new-fangled flying machines. Which, I guess, it was. The second thing is a little different." He pulled a dog-eared deck of cards out of his pocket and gave it a few quick shuffles and cuts, then fanned it open under my nose. "Here, pick a card."

"Information first," I told him. "Card tricks later."

"Pick a card," he insisted.

I picked a card. It was the eight of hearts. "Now what?"

Tom closed his eyes. "Eight of hearts," he said "Another."

I pulled another card. The two of spades.

"Deuce of spades. Here, you take the deck."

I took the deck and shuffled it. Then I pulled a card from the middle and took a look. The king of clubs.

Tom frowned. Then he smiled. "King of clubs."

"Very clever," I said. "What's the gimmick, a marked deck?"

"I don't know," Tom said. "Try again."

"Let me," Sylvia suggested, pulling a card from the deck.

"Four of clubs," Tom said after a moment.

"I haven't looked at it," Sylvia said. "And I've been cupping it in my hand so you couldn't read the markings."

"Look," Tom said.

Sylvia looked at the card. "It's the four of clubs," she said. "How do you do it? Or is this another of your magician's secrets?"

"I tell you I don't know. I've been able to predict cards perfectly ever since I got here. The skill doesn't seem to extend to other areas, unfortunately. Maybe if I had a better idea of just what the skill was, I could use it better."

"Let me try," I said. The deck was shuffled, and Sylvia picked a card, which I didn't guess. We tried it three more times, with the same results. Then Tom picked. I still couldn't guess. "It's either a freak ability activated by your arrival on this world, or it's something in the nature of this world itself which you're able to utilize this way because of your long interest in cards and card tricks," I analyzed.

"Perhaps it's a poltergeist," Tom suggested.

"Rah-di-do," I agreed.

Sylvia said, "That's all very nice, but what do we do next?"

"I have a theory," Tom said. "I've been thinking over your story while I was giving readings, and something's occurred to me,"

"Spill it," I said.

"We all seem to have blipped, if I may borrow the term . . ."

"It's all yours," I assured him.

". . . at moments of crisis. Or shortly after moments of crisis. This would seem to indicate that the phenomenon is brought about by human beings in some way, and at particular moments. Also, either that only certain human beings—like us—are likely to cause this thing, or that people have very few moments of crisis."

"Not all of them happened during a crisis," I protested.

"No? Think back. Once you were being chased by a flying saucer, once by an angry mob, once by a bunch of tanks. I was trapped inside of a misbegotten trunk."

"The mob was already well behind us," I protested.

"Maybe the blip had to catch up to the train. Maybe there were some waiting ahead of you that you didn't know about. How do I know? I still say the blips are caused by people, or at least activated by people, in times of crisis."

"What about Sylvia's circus train?"

"Maybe it was about to crack up."

"Boy, what you won't do to support a shaky theory."

"Have you got a better one?"

"No," I admitted.

"I'll take it one step further," Tom continued.

"I was afraid you would."

"Each blip," Tom said, ignoring me, "takes us closer to the heart of the trouble, whatever it is."

"How do you figure that?" I asked.

"It seems reasonable. At least, we all seem to be going in the same direction. You and I, for example, quite separately arrived here. Also, as you tell it, in each world you've passed through there've been more and more, um, travelers."

"That's been true up to now," I admitted. "But we haven't seen any here except you."

"Yes," Tom said. "But this is Ogallala, Nebraska. How do we know what's happening in New York, or even Omaha?"

"A touch," I admitted. "A distinct touch."

"So, what we have to do is get as quickly as possible through as many blips as we can cause."

I said, "Now that's . . . Wait a minute; did you say 'find' or 'cause'?"

"Cause. Cause. Don't wait for them to come to you, go to them. Besides, crises we cause ourselves are likely to be safer than ones that hunt you up."

"I'm not sure I like this," I said. "Couldn't we just go out and get swallowed up by some nice flying saucer?"

"It might come to that," Tom assured me cheerfully.

Sylvia stared intently at us. "I'm not sure I understand."

"You're lucky," I told her. "Don't bother trying. This nut wants to get us killed."

"Why?" she asked Tom.

"Michael always exaggerates these things," Tom told her. "He also beats his women and eats crackers in bed."

"He does not!" Sylvia defended me.

"If you want to beat her," I told Tom, "I'd suggest using a damn long whip. You've never seen her in action."

"After what you've told me," Tom assured me, "I intend to stay very friendly with your little girl. And I intend to do this from a reasonable distance."

"You make fun of me," Sylvia said sharply.

"No, no, not at all," we assured her in unison.

"Bah!" she said. "Keep your clown act for that vaudeville you killed. Let's get busy and do something."

"Just what I was about to propose," Tom said.

"Yes? What did you have in mind?"

"We're going to do a little high-wire act in the big top. The show just went on."

"You're crazy!" I said firmly. "I freely admit that for me to get on one of those high wires would cause a crisis, but I don't think I'd live through it."

"That's not exactly what I meant," Tom said. "Just stay here for a minute; I'll be right back." He headed toward the back of the cook tent with the purposeful stride of a man with a mission.

"What's all this?" Sylvia asked me.

"I'm not sure," I told her. "How are you on the high wire?"

"Wire walking? It's simple. Any child of ten can do it—with about fourteen years practice."

"You're very reassuring," I said. "Oh, well. You only live however many times you manage to live."

Tom came back with two large wicker baskets under his arm. "Here, take one of these," he said. "Come on along."

I took one of the baskets and we went to the rear of the big top and entered through a canvas tunnel. We emerged on the sawdust, surrounded by the tiers of paying customers. The house seemed to be almost full. An animal act and a brace of acrobats were performing on the floor, while a couple of aerialists warmed up overhead. My nostrils filled with the familiar smell of circus, mingled with the unfamiliar odor of incipient panic. I didn't think I was going to like whatever Tom was leading us into.

"There; the platform halfway up that tent pole," Tom said, pointing to the nearer of the two. "Just head for the rope like you know what you're doing and nobody will stop you. Then climb it to the tower. We'll go one at a time."

"First of all," I informed Tom, "I can't climb a rope, at least not that high. Second of all, I sure as hell can't climb a rope with this mother of all baskets in my hand."

"Right," Tom said. "I forgot about that. The basket, I mean. You can climb the rope because it's not just a rope, it's a rope ladder. As for the baskets, there's a pulley rope attached to the platform for lifting equipment. I'll go first and tie my basket to the bottom of the rope. Then, when I get to the top, I can pull it up while Sylvia's climbing. Then I'll lower it, and you can tie your basket on the end, and I'll pull that up while you're climbing. Got it?"

Sylvia nodded. I think she was so thrilled at being back in a circus that she didn't care what we were going to do. I also nodded, but not quite as happily.

Tom stalked across the sawdust like he owned the place and went up the rope. Sylvia danced over and floated effortlessly up the rope, the ascending basket bobbing a few feet over her head. I walked over to the pole, sure that every eye in the place was riveted to me and that any second somebody that knew I had no business there was going to bar my way and order me out. The only thing that barred my way was an elephant who seemed to have decided that he liked one of the girl acrobats, and was following her around the ring. The audience broke into a fit of giggles and applauded, so I decided that not quite all of them were looking at me. I reached the pole, tied the basket on to the dangling end of rope which dropped to me, and started up the ladder. It swayed with every step and kept me at an angle which forced me to look at the very top of the tent. As I got higher I felt more and more visible and more and more alone. There was a hushed silence, and I was sure the crowd was waiting for me to fall; then loud cheering broke out, and I thought I had started to fall. Then I was at the top and Sylvia was helping me to clamber onto the platform. "Well," I said, "is *that* all there is to it?"

"Sit down," Tom said, "and help me open the baskets."

"Sure," I said. I squatted over one of the baskets and undid the wicker catches, swinging the top open. The thing was full of food: apples, tomatoes, oranges, eggs, grapefruit and assorted other goodies.

Tom was busy in the other corner. "What are you doing?" I asked him. "And what's this stuff for?"

"I'm pulling up the ladder," Tom said.

"Just as I thought," I said. "You're preparing for a siege. How long do you think we can hold out here before we run out of food?"

"We'll be out of food very shortly," Tom said. "Don't think of it as food; think of it as a supply of missiles."

"Missiles?"

"Right. Objects to be thrown."

Sylvia picked up a tomato. "Thrown? At whom?"

"Them," Tom said, waving his hand around. "The crowd. The rubes. The audience. All of them."

"You're crazy," I reiterated. "They'll lynch us."

"Yes, but they'll have to get at us first, and that's not going to be too easy. That's why I picked up here."

"And our getaway? You've planned that too, of course."

"I know of no way to get out of here," Tom said. "I figure that if I did, it wouldn't be a real crisis." He picked an egg up and hefted it in his hand. "We've got to pick the spots where they'll do the most good. Places where they're all jammed together, so you've got to hit someone. If you're lucky, more than one."

"You," I told him. "Not me. I'm not going to have any part of this."

"Try convincing them," Tom said. He lobbed the egg out in an easy overhand toss.

"Say," Sylvia said. "This is fun." I noticed that the tomato was gone from her hand, and now she held an orange.

"Oh, well," I said. "If I'm going to be hung for a sheep, I might as well get a few lamb chops." I picked up an apple and heaved it into the mass of people in front of me. There was no reaction, so I decided to try to aim, picking a bald head in the crowd as my target. I missed, but several people to his left looked up, so I had an idea where it went. I tried to correct.

Sylvia was pitching them out with a powerful sidearm toward a tight group of middle-aged ladies in print dresses. Tom was lobbing them out over a wide area. "What we need," he remarked, "is a Norden bombsight."

The first puzzled murmur ran through the crowd. Several people stood up and began screaming unhearable epithets while mopping themselves off. People behind them stood up to shush them.

The activity in the rings drew to a halt as one performer after another spotted what was happening and stopped to stare at us. This triggered the audience, and they found us. We kept lobbing the overripe fruit and eggs while the sporadic shouting turned into a steady growl, and then a roar.

A couple of performers raced over to the pole and looked around, puzzled, for the rope ladder. Then they ran over to the other pole and began climbing that. Tom busied himself with removing the wire stretched between the two, so he wouldn't have to do it with someone on it. We kept throwing.

The crowd began to surge back and forth like water in a bathtub. The performers tried to keep them back, but there were far too few, and they disappeared in the wave of people. Some of the audience were heading for the walls of the tent, interested only in getting out as quickly as possible; but most were headed for us.

We didn't have to throw now, we could just drop. The crowd gathered around the pole, and the screaming quickly reached a frenzied pitch.

The pole began to sway slightly. The sides of the tent started to collapse, uprooted by the people pushing their way under them. Then the lights went out.

By now it was like being in a crow's-nest in a hurricane; the platform swayed from side to side in ever-wider arcs, and gave a sharp little clicking sound at the farpoint of each sway.

There was a snapping sound as one of the guyed wires gave way, and the platform headed for the ground. Canvas folded around us.

# BLIP

# 9

The canvas had disappeared. The pole had disappeared. The people had disappeared. The circus had disappeared.

We were falling.

I hit ice-cold water and sank deeper and longer than I believed possible. Then I stopped sinking and realized that I had no air in my lungs. I clawed my way to the surface and popped up, gasping. Sylvia was a few yards away, looking like a wet puppy but apparently unhurt. She reached me with a few strokes and we clung to each other until we had to come up for air.

"Where's Tom?" she asked, treading water like a seal.

"I don't care," I said, looking around. "I hope the idiot drowns. Tom! Tom! Are you all right? I don't see him, he might be in trouble." I dove under and fished around, without even finding bottom, and came up for air. Tom was up by then, and making a lusty dogpaddle for shore. Sylvia and I set after him, and soon the three of us were lying, exhausted, in the grass.

After I had gathered sufficient breath, I sat up. "You nincompoop!" I said. "What a plan. You almost get us killed by a collapsing tent, and when we do blip it leaves us forty feet in the air. Thank God it was over a lake."

"I had, er, overlooked that possibility," Tom said. "You had more experience with this sort of thing, why didn't you tell me? I sort of assumed we'd arrive on the ground."

"If you'd told me what you had in mind," I said. I lay back down. "Forget it. We're alive. Wet, but alive."

A deep bass voice said, "Pardon me, gentlemen," and we all looked around. We were surrounded by a semicircle of breastplate-clad soldiery. Sylvia sprang to her feet while Tom and I pushed ourselves into more-or-less sitting positions.

"Pardon me," the bass-voiced sergeant-at-arms went on. "Lady and gentlemen. My mistake, but it was only a fleeting glimpse we had of you as you fell. We, hem, saw your arrival, you see."

"Don't ask me to explain it," Tom said. "I don't understand it either."

"I assure you, sir, that no explanations are necessary, at least, not to me. However, I have orders to request that all, hem, visitors like yourselves allow themselves to be interviewed by higher authority."

"Request?" I asked, standing up and putting my arm around Sylvia.

"Oh, of course," the sergeant said, sounding shocked.

"Suppose we don't want to go?" Tom asked.

"But where else would you go?" the sergeant replied. "You have no money, no jobs, no living quarters; and here someone wants to provide them all in return for a little information. I assure you you won't be mistreated in any way. The lord just wants to gather together as much information on the visitors we've been getting recently, to see if he can find the cause of the, hem, problem. Now, wouldn't *you* like to know the cause of all this?"

"What lord?" Tom asked.

"Why, Lord Gart himself, of course. But then, you wouldn't know about himself, or any of us, being visitors as you are. Come along with us, and by this time tomorrow you'll be meeting him yourself more than likely. We'll pick up dry clothes for you at the first post station."

We glanced at one another, and I shrugged and nodded. We might as well go; we might learn something. Besides, with the force of men they had, if they planned any nastiness they wouldn't have to trick us into it. At least they'd think so, not knowing of my wonder girl and her flying feet.

We rode double horseback, each of us behind a trooper, to the first post station, about five miles away. There we were given clean, dry clothes, fed, and bundled into a closed coach for the rest of the journey.

The trip was very efficiently arranged. At each post station we stopped to change teams and were given enough time to stretch our legs and relieve ourselves. The driver and his assistant were changed at every third post. We rode right through the night. In the morning we picked up a hamper of breakfast and continued.

"What do you think?" Tom asked, picking at a chicken leg.

"About what?" I inquired.

"About poltergeists," he responded. "Do you really think they constitute the principal types of psychical manifestations?"

"What's that?" Sylvia was interested.

"It's his way of being clever," I told her. "The next bit in the act is to sing 'George Washington Bridge' for you. If you ignore him, he'll go away."

"That's right," Tom assured her, "I leave in a huff. A large, cream-colored huff."

"Oh."

"What do I think about what?" I reinquired.

"What's going to happen to us at the other end of this carriage ride."

"We're going to be questioned, fed, clothed and sheltered."

"Like POW's. What do we tell them, name, rank and serial number?"

I thought about it. "I guess not. I think we should tell Lord Gart the whole story. Since he has such an elaborate setup to receive visitors, he obviously has some idea of what's happening. Maybe we can sort of trade information; it might help us."

"I lean toward agreeing with you," Tom said. "But I have a suspicious mind. We'd better stay on the alert."

"I thought," Sylvia interjected, "that we'd agreed to that last night."

"We always repeat ourselves," I told her. "It's our trademark."

The coach made one more pitstop before the end of the trip. It was early afternoon when we drove into the courtyard of a big manor house. The coachman swung down from his perch and opened the door for us. "Milady, gentlemen, we've arrived. Please step down."

As we descended from the coach, a young, uniformed man hurried down the steps to greet us. "Are these the latest?" he asked the coachman, who tipped his hat respectfully.

"They are, sir."

"You made good time. Greetings. We received word on the teleson to expect you. Please follow me."

He turned and led us up the steps, through the massive oak doors, through a large reception hall and into a room. During the walk I tried to place the costume. The closest I could come was British Navy at about the time of the Napoleonic Wars. "Please take seats," he said. "Someone will come for you in a few minutes." Giving us a cross between a nod and a salute, he left.

The room we were in was bare except for the Persian rug centered on the floor and a lot of straight-back chairs with embroidered seats scattered around, backs to the wall. The floor sticking out around the edges of the rug was highly polished wood. The walls were papered in a patterned, high-textured red, and decorated with Famous Ancestor paintings. We sat in three chairs close to the door to do our waiting.

I put my arm around Sylvia, who was looking glum. "Cheer up," I said, "everything's going to be all right."

"Do you swear it?" she asked earnestly.

"I do," I told her. "Just stick with me, kid."

Tom took out his pipe and tamped tobacco down into its maw. He lit it with that serious, cross-eyed expression common to all true pipe-smokers. "Tell me," he said. "Any new thoughts about our condition?"

"Well," I said. "We're in the hands of the military. That could be either good or bad, we'll have to wait and see. And I wonder what a teleson is."

"I agree," Tom said.

Sylvia asked, "Why do you think so?"

"We've been treated with military efficiency throughout," I told her. "I'll bet even the drivers were plainclothes EM. Besides, it's the old military pattern: hurry up and wait."

"EM?" Sylvia asked.

"Enlisted men. In this case probably NCO's, or non-commissioned officers to you."

An old man, who by his costume was either a high functionary or a butler, hobbled in. "Good afternoon," he said. "Please come with me." We came: around a corner, up a wide flight of stairs, around another corner, down a long hallway and into a room.

There, behind a compact desk, sat a heavily gold-braided naval officer. He stood as we entered the room. "Please take seats." We did, and he sat. "Good afternoon. Welcome to the Angevin Empire. I am Captain LeClerk, chief of naval intelligence for New England. I am in charge of what we are calling Project Visitor, directly under Lord Gart. You'll be staying here, under my charge, until we're done with you: probably no more than a couple of days. Then you're free to go, with the one restriction that we'd appreciate it if you didn't discuss your travels through time, or whatever it turns out to be, with our natives. They're a superstitious bunch, and your story is quite liable to make them think you're agents of the Devil. We've checked, if you're interested, and as far as we can determine there is no diabolic influence involved.

"We will, of course, try to maintain a paternal influence when you leave: see to suitable housing, employment and the like. We're even now setting up an indoctrination course to acquaint those of you whose lives were especially dissimilar to ours with our customs, habits and laws. First let me take down your names, then I'll try to answer any questions you might have." He picked up a quill pen and looked inquiringly at us.

"Michael Kurland," I told him.

"Kurland," he repeated. "Polish?"

"No, American."

"I just wondered. We're having a little dispute with the Polish Empire right now. It wouldn't have affected you in any case. I would have just had to warn you not to speak Polish around here; you'd keep getting turned in for a spy."

"Thomas Waters," Tom said.

The officer wrote it. "Waters. Waters? Well, well, isn't that interesting." Tom looked puzzled.

"Lady Sylvia DuChamp," Sylvia said.

"Well," he said, writing it down. "Welcome, Lady DuChamp. You're our first noble visitor."

"Just Lady Sylvia," she told him. "You do know the distinction?"

"Of course. Welcome, Lady Sylvia. Now, any questions?"

"You seem to think we're going to settle here," I said. "What makes you think we'll be here that long?"

"You'll be free to go anywhere you like," he said. "I just assumed you'd want to stay here at least until you got to know our world."

"That," I told him, "isn't what I meant. We've already passed through several worlds, involuntarily, I assure you. If the pattern holds true, we won't be here more than a few days."

Captain LeClerk looked startled. "Several worlds? More than one? By the Good Lord, that's something! You're the first, you know. Through more than one world, the chief will be fascinated. You really are travelers. We must get your histories at once." He rang a small, brass bell on his desk. "Bocco will show you to your rooms. I'd appreciate it if you'd write down a summary of your travels for us, putting in everything you think relevant. You do know how to write?"

We assured him that we did.

"Splendid. Even you, Lady Sylvia? Splendid. Dinner will be in about three hours. If you could have something ready by then, it would give Lord Gart a chance to go over it. I'm sure he'll want to see you after dinner. We'll see what we can do about clothing for you; give you a chance to change into something fresh. I'm afraid it'll be some uniform or another for the men, and we'll do the best we can for you, milady. We've ordered a stock of clothing to accommodate future visitors, but it's been arriving in dribs and drabs, mostly, I'm afraid, drabs. Whoever put in the first order must have been thinking of garbing prisoners. But I've done what I can to set that aright."

Bocco, our functionary/butler, appeared at the door.

"Bocco, please show these gentlemen, and Lady Sylvia, to their rooms. They'll be taking dinner in the Blue Room."

Bocco seemed subtly impressed, either by Lady Sylvia or the Blue Room, or possibly both. Our rooms were one flight up and adjoined: Lady Sylvia in one and Tom and I in the next. We opened the connecting door and gathered in Sylvia's room to talk.

"Lady Sylvia," Tom said. "You didn't tell me."

"Didn't tell me, either," I added.

"Were you putting him on?"

"Putting him . . ."

"Fooling or tricking him," I explained.

"Oh, no indeed. I am Lady Sylvia. My father is Lord Farthing."

"Not Lord DuChamp?" Tom asked.

"That's not the way it works. Don't you have titles in your world?"

"In our world, yes. But not on our continent. As a result, I've noticed that people in our country seem much more impressed with titles."

"Well, my father is Henry DuChamp, Lord Farthing. He has loads of additional names strung in there with a few extra titles, but they only come out on state occasions."

I asked, "What's the bit about your only being Lady Sylvia? Why not Lady DuChamp or Lady Farthing?"

"My mother is Lady Farthing, as the lord's wife. If a woman inherits the title, say if my older brother dies, then I'd be Lady Farthing. Whoever I married wouldn't be Lord Farthing, but only Lord Michael, for example. There's more like that; every situation you can think of has been covered, and probably happened once or twice."

"I'm sure," I said.

"Well," Tom said, "let's get to writing. It's the least we can do for our hosts." We retired to our separate writing desks, or secretaries, or whatever you call them.

"Look!" Tom called, waving the top sheet of his pile of stationery in the air. "Genuine foolscap. The stuff Dickens used."

"How can you tell?" I asked him.

"It looks like foolscap. It feels like foolscap. It says 'foolscap' on the watermark. I shall create a masterpiece."

"Call it *Oliver Twist,*" I suggested, buckling down to work. I started with the quill and inkwell supplied, and succeeded only in thoroughly smudging a sheet of paper. Slow-drying inks are not meant for left-handed people. Either your hand follows what you write, smudging it beyond recognition and messing up your hand, or you hold your hand twisted around above the line you're writing, and the words look like hentracks. Sighing a mighty sigh, I crumpled the top sheet and threw it away. Then I remembered a felt-tip I had collapsed in my wallet, and pulled it out.

I went into a creative trance for a few minutes before setting felt to paper, then started writing. The words flowed on to the paper as I remembered people and events. The thing I had to watch, I found as I crossed out words, was the temptation to use similes that wouldn't be understood here.

Tom stretched and stamped his feet. "I wish I had a Pepsi," he said, "or even a Moxie. I can't write without a soda."

"Ring for the butler," I suggested. "I wish I had lined paper, or a typewriter."

"Where would you plug it in?" Tom asked.

"There is such a thing as a non-electric typewriter."

"Sure, and there used to be wind-up phonographs too; but why settle, especially as long as you're wishing. Always wish for the best, that's my motto."

"I thought your motto was 'Poltergeists constitute the principal types of psychical manifestations,'" I said. "Or, alternatively, that sign you used to have above your typewriter: 'An appealing character strives against overwhelming odds to achieve a worthwhile goal.'"

"One adapts one's motto to fit one's needs. Besides, I remember the sign above your typewriter: 'Boy meets girl, boy loses girl, boy builds girl.' You're nothing but a dirty android-lover."

"You're just jealous because you can't afford a girl of your own, with all the latest attachments," I told him.

"Pah!" he said. "You science-fiction writers are all the same. No imagination."

Recess over, we went back to writing. The butler arrived with clothes for us, which he distributed to the right places. Tom attempted to describe his beverage needs to him, and he hurried away, promising to try. A short while later, a lesser functionary, in a less glorious costume, arrived with corked bottles of what proved to be a very good sparkling cider.

After completing our literary efforts, which were collected by a junior officer, we washed up at sink stands. These were wooden pieces of furniture with porcelain sink bowls and a stopper and drain, which I discovered led to a pail hidden by wooden double doors. The sinks were filled from a pitcher of water set by the stand. The soap was of very good quality, except that it tended to dissolve a bit too readily and smelled of exotic oils.

The clothing we received were navy dress uniforms; or, I suppose, in this world of elaborate costumes only semi-dress uniforms, complete to gold-trimmed epaulettes. "I wonder what rank I am," I said, admiring myself as I put on the heavy jacket.

"Probably 'Distinguished Visitor, Second Class,'" Tom guessed. "Most navies have a uniform provision for that sort of thing."

"I suppose you're right," I said.

"Sorry to spoil your daydreams. No leading ships of the line into battle against the Spanish—or, I guess here, Polish—Armada. No standing firm on the quarterdeck, issuing orders in an iron voice while cannonballs pierce the air around you and the deck under you. No getting yourself heroically killed to earn a few lines in the *Naval Gazette*: 'Commodore Theodore Bear distinguished himself in an action on the Seventeenth on the Cape of Good Hope. He was killed immediately before the engagement terminated, but had succeeded in capturing two enemy vessels, one of which sank from internal damage before it could reach port. Commodore Bear's final command was executed in a manner that exemplifies the best traditions of the Angevin Navy, and he is to be posthumously knighted and to receive the Order of the Angevin Empire. In ceremonies to take place on the Fifth, Mrs. Bear will receive the O.A.E. for her late husband.'"

"It would have looked good," I said.

"What would have looked good?"

"The O.A.E. I wonder if you pin it to your chest or wear it around your neck. It's a shame I had to die before I got it."

"Shut up," Tom said. "You'll make me cry."

Someone in the place must have been Sylvia's size, because the dinner gown they found for her fit like it had been painted on. It was red, low cut and floor length; and that's all I can tell you about it, being a man and not knowing the terms. Her hair was combed back into long, flowing waves down to her shoulders, and she looked beautiful. That, being a man, I can affirm. A thin strand of pearls complimented the dress and her skin. She glowed.

"You," I told her as she came through the connecting door, "look beautiful."

"I feel beautiful," she said. "They really know the proper way to treat a woman here. I've had a wonderfully scented bath, which I must have stayed in for half an hour, and a maid came in to help me dress and make up."

"You're using make-up?" I asked, inspecting her.

"It's not supposed to show, only to highlight," she told me. "The maid showed me how they do it here."

"Will I ruin anything if I kiss you?" I asked.

"I sincerely hope not," she said. "Let's see." Carefully, so as not to crease her dress, we embraced.

"Okay, lovebirds," Tom called after a while, "break it up, we have to go down to dinner."


The blue room was magnificent; richly draped, full of the deep colors of ancient wood and ornately furnished and decorated. It was lit by both gas and candle, the gas mantles glowing with a pure white brightness. That pleased me, as I don't like eating in the dark. Dimly lit restaurants always make me think they're trying to hide the food.

Lord Gart sat in a heavy chair at the head of the large table that dominated the room. He was already seated when the rest of us entered. He rose about three inches from the chair to acknowledge the ladies, then planked down again. We filed around the table and sat down, ladies, of course, first.

Lord Gart was massive, both in height and girth. He made the rest of us look like children sitting down to eat with daddy. His arms were large, his chest was large, his belly held the weight of many meals; resting on top of a thick, short neck, was a head that almost dwarfed the rest. Thick brown hair curled about the top of it, and a dark, heavy, square-cut beard, tinged with grey, framed the square face. His close-set eyes, under bushy brows, radiated intelligence and interest in all that went on around him, while the rest of his face, from thick lips to large, close-set ears, was constantly animated by the emotions that passed under the creased brow.

To his right sat a tall, gaunt, ascetic-looking man, whose thin white hair was neatly plastered down in all directions over his high-domed head. He had large, grey, inquiring eyes that seemed to possess the quality of being able to look inside whatever his gaze rested on. They were set well apart, and separated by the prominent, angular nose of a friendly eagle. His plain grey-white robes provided mass contrast to the linear and pointal splendor of Lord Gart's crimson, blue, gold, and snow-white raiment. This was Sir Thomas Leseaux, Fellow of the Imperial College of Thaumaturgy, Master of the Guild of Sorcerers, and chief advisor and close friend of Lord Gart. He was, so Captain LeClerk whispered to us, his vowels rounded by awe, the leading theoretical thaumaturgist in the empire.

To his right sat the Demoiselle Tia, a short dark-haired beauty who was engaged to Sir Thomas and was, so rumor had it, one of the best natural witches in the business. I merely quote what I was told.

We sat across and further down the table, flanked and fronted by naval officers and their women, with an occasional guardsman or civilian thrown in for leaven. If it sounds like the table was large, it doesn't exaggerate. I might add that the chairs were roomy, and by no means crowded together. After removing the crustation of silver and linen, the table could have been used as two lanes in a bowling alley.

Using the noise of the soup course to hide my words, I leaned toward Sylvia. Pitching my voice so that it would just reach Tom, on her other side, I asked, "What do you think about all this sorcery and witchcraft business? Isn't that carrying the middle ages motif a little far?"

"Let's wait before we make any judgments," Tom said. "All we've heard so for are the words, we don't know what they mean to these people yet. You've got to expect a few linguistic differences."

"That's true," I admitted and, feeling a bit reassured, went back to my soup.

The conversation was fragmented, uninhibited, and ran a bit to the sanguine. Two men to my right were holding a running argument as to whether one could or could not cut off a standing man's head with a single one-handed swipe of a cavalry saber. An elderly naval type across the table was holding forth to anyone who would listen on the Battle of the Sea of Crete. That was back in '32, when he was a junior lieutenant on the *Coeur de Lion,* flagship of the Mediterranean Fleet, under Admiral of the Red, Sir Arthur Welsley.

After telling the story for thirty years, he had finally turned it into an epic poem, which he recited at full bellow, with appropriate table thumping. I remember the ending:

> *Though the decks ran red with the sea-washed blood,*
> *And the mainmast cleft in twain;*
> *Still the guns ran out to the quarterdeck shout*
> *And rent the seas again.*
>
> *The ensign shouted load while the Admiral strode*
> *Down the deck with his white cockade*
> *And inspected each gun with the calm of one*
> *On a Sunday dress parade.*
>
> *Now the enemy spoke with a mighty throat,*
> *And the balls went whistling past.*
> *And we replied with our last broadside,*
> *And choked on the smoke it cast.*
>
> *Then the smoke had cleared, and a few men cheered*
> *As our enemy burst apart*
> *But more men prayed for that white cockade*
> *Above the Admiral's splattered heart.*

"Splattered heart?" one of the women was brave enough to ask.

"Actually," the poet confided, "he was hit by a cannonball. It turned him to grape jelly all over, but I couldn't fit that into the meter."

"Oh," the woman said, turning green and putting down her fork.

Lord Gart, I noticed, wasn't eating much, but he was drinking like a man with a secret stomach. His conversation dominated the table, not because anyone deferred to him, but simply because he had a voice like a tuba in full throat. He was discoursing on heraldry, and throwing around words like gules, argent, rampant, file, lozenge and the like. I thought I knew what most of the words meant, but the way he strung them together made no sense to me. I later learned a little about it, but still didn't see the point. If your family crest is a silver dragon pawing the air on a red shield, why can't you say that instead of "Gules, a dragon rampant, argent."

Everyone disbursed without much formality after dinner. We were asked to stick around, as Lord Gart would want to see us shortly. He didn't keep us waiting.

His office was large and severely functional. It was dominated by a great desk in one corner and by Lord Gart himself, sitting behind the desk. The office walls were covered with books, stacked and piled on ceiling-high shelves. Flanking Lord Gart, left and right, were Sir Thomas Leseaux and Captain LeClerk.

Lord Gart waved us into three seats facing the desk while he leafed through our writings and steadily swigged from a flagon of wine on the desk. Wine and brandy were his steady companions, but he never seemed in the least affected by them. It was as if his huge body burned alcohol as its rightful fuel. "Fascinating," he said. "Utterly fascinating. Don't you agree, Master Thomas?"

Sir Thomas Leseaux nodded thoughtfully. "It clears up several points," he agreed in a crisp, clear tenor that would have held its own in any company but Lord Gart's. "We have a variety of theories prepared," he explained, "which will fit all the facts we are aware of. One of them is most certainly right, and we're working out test procedures for the most likely. Every new bit of information we gather is of great use in either clarifying or eliminating some of our theoretical structures. Your stories will be of even greater utility, as they will help us establish the overall pattern in finer detail. We have many questions to ask, and I hope you'll bear with me."

"We'll be glad to do anything we can to help," Tom said. "I wonder if you could tell me . . ."

Sir Thomas held up his hand. "Please. I, in turn, will be glad to answer all your questions; but allow me to conduct the first interrogation."

We nodded, and the questioning began. Most of the questions covered the times immediately before and after each blip, but a few of them ranged pretty far afield. Lord Gart showed a deep interest in as much information on the size, weight and speed of the Tiger tanks that attacked us as I could dredge out of my memory. Sir Thomas sent out for a variety of fabrics, and had Tom pick the one that most closely corresponded to the tent canvas that had collapsed around us. All of them asked questions from every possible angle about the flying saucers. As the French say, it marched.

The last part of the intensive quiz (worth a total of ten points, answer in brief sentences) was basically semantic. Sir Thomas recited a list of words and had each of us explain fully what every word meant, objectively and subjectively. Try it for fun sometime. Some of the words were: religion, chance, luck, magic, truth, science and country.

After this ordeal, Lord Gart leaned back and laced his fingers behind his head. "That seems to be it," he said. "I thank you for your patience; you must have felt like felons before the bench during some of that questioning."

"More like a doctoral candidate going up for his orals," I replied. Sir Thomas chuckled.

"Turn about is fair play, as a lady of my acquaintance keeps insisting," Lord Gart boomed. "What can we tell you? It's getting late, so we'll hold lengthy explanations until tomorrow; but is there anything we can answer now?"

"Well," I said, "my basic question is simply what's going up, but I guess that will have to keep."

"If you mean in regard to the time-track hopping you seem to have developed a propensity for; I may have a partial answer for you tomorrow," Sir Thomas said. "I'm working, you may be interested to know, with a fellow refugee like yourselves; a Dr. Immanuel Capabella. He comes from a time track much like your own, perhaps you've heard of him?"

We shook our heads, no.

"Ah, well. One track this side or the other, it's hard to tell. No matter. One thing I can tell you. No, two things. One: this is what you would call a problem of parallel time tracks, only they seem to have become slightly acute. Two: this problem is a serious threat to us all; not only to those who have track-hopped, or those on this timeline, but the whole infinite universe of six-dimensional continuums in the immediate area of the sun, our star. It will probably encompass several of the local stars also, and may cover the entire galaxy we call the Milky Way. I doubt it can spread any farther, though."

"That," I said, "is reassuring."

"One other thing," Tom said. "All this reference we keep hearing to what you refer to as magic. What do you mean by the word?"

"Harumph!" Lord Gart snorted. "Your turn, Sir Thomas. Let's hear you do a little defining for a change."

Sir Thomas smiled. "I'm very much afraid that we mean the same thing you do by the term. Real magic, you understand; not stage illusion, sleight of hand, or other forms of trickery. The magic your prestidigitators and illusionists are trying to sham. The magic of Sulayman the Wise, of Merlin and the great monk Johannes Magnus. That is what we mean by magic.

"But there is one important difference between our uses of the word. You see, here in our world, the world of the Angevin Empire, a world that split off from yours so long ago that we still have a Plantagenet on the throne, there is an additional factor. Magic works!"

We were silent for a moment after that bombshell, and then Tom spoke up. "What, exactly, do you mean?"

Lord Gart slapped his palm down on the desk. "Just that, my lad," he growled. "Just that. What your world calls a bunch of superstitious crap, beg pardon my Lady, which anyone who claims to practice is a charlatan. This excepts stage magicians and illusionists, which we also have, who do not so much claim their feats are magic as defy you to show they're not. At any rate, what on your world is considered superstitious, ah, balderdash, is on ours—here—known as the Art of the Possible. Magic works so well for us that we've never had to develop that hodgepodge of smelly machines that you call science."

"Yes," Tom said, looking at me and then back at Lord Gart. "I see."

"You don't believe?" Lord Gart asked. "You are, naturally, incredulous. No matter, the working of magic does not depend on your belief." He waved a pudgy finger. "Can you show them, Sir Thomas?"

Sir Thomas Leseaux placed his hands together before his nose. "That, um, is not entirely accurate, my Lord. A lot of magic is, very definitely, dependent upon belief."

Tom smiled.

"But," Sir Thomas said, leaning forward, "a good bit of it isn't. Take for example, Mr. Waters, the extraordinary predictive powers you suddenly developed over a deck of playing cards." Sir Thomas snapped his fingers. "That ties it in! Of course, how blind of me. That's the final factor."

"We don't consider that magic," Tom said. "We call it telepathy."

Leseaux stared at him contemplatively for a minute. "So you give it a name and that makes it scientific. All right, name this." He took a brass tray from the desk and tossed it to Tom.

"What do you mean?" Tom asked. "It's a tray."

"Yes," Sir Thomas said, taking a short, stubby wand from his sleeve. "Remember, I'm only a theoretical thaumaturgist; I usually leave this sort of thing to others. But we'll give it a try." He muttered something while tracing an intricate pattern in the air with his wand. "Now, toss it back."

Tom shrugged and gave the tray a discus toss back.

Sir Thomas pointed the wand. *"Rama!"*

The tray froze in midair, suspended four feet off the floor between Tom and the desk. We stared at it.

"*Replax!*" Sir Thomas said sharply, and the tray slowly settled back down on the desk. "That's it, I'm afraid," he said. "Not very impressive."

"It'll do," I said. "We, um, thank you for the demonstration."

With that the meeting broke up and we went back to our rooms. Tom was unusually silent.

# 10

The next morning after breakfast, we received an invitation to join Sir Thomas in his laboratory behind the main house. As we approached we saw him standing in the doorway patiently listening to a short, paunchy man in a white bowler hat covered with arcane symbols.

"The apprentice problem," the man yelled, punctuating his remarks by jabbing the air in front of him. "Incredible, simply incredible. After two years in the shop, this colt can't even work out a simple problem in the Law of Similarity. He gets mad at me one night, see; so he takes this wax doll from stock—right off the shelf. He daubs a little of my hair and stuff, even a couple of drops of blood from where I cut myself over the workbench. Says what *he* thinks are the right spells over it, then snaps off the right arm."

"Malicious," Sir Thomas said.

"Yeah, but stupid. How do you think I find out? By breaking my arm? By even getting a pain in my arm? No. The next morning I walk into the shop and find all the *other* wax dolls have their arms broken. The nincompoop got the spell backward."

"You were lucky," Sir Thomas commented.

"Lucky! I put a spell of *non conjunctous* on the ungrateful brat and sent him back where he came from. Now I have to start interviewing apprentices again. Two years shot. Oh, well. Thanks for the formulary," he patted an ancient brown book under his arm. "I'll get it back to you as soon as I can."

"No hurry," Sir Thomas said. The little man gave him a quick handshake and trotted off down the path.

"Good morning," we called, walking up to the door.

"Ah. Good morning to you. I hope you slept well. Lady Sylvia, I have a surprise for you."

"A surprise?" Sylvia looked pleased. "What sort of surprise?"

"Something that arrived late yesterday. I didn't find out until this morning. The Demoiselle Tia will take you over to it." He turned his head and called, "Tia! Come out here."

The short, black-haired girl came, almost skipping, out of a back room. "Hello," she said. "I've been talking to the frogs."

"The frogs?" I asked.

"Yes. Sir Thomas has cages and cages of frogs inside. They don't like being caged up, so I go in and talk to them sometimes; to cheer them up, you know."

"Oh," I said.

Sir Thomas looked with affection on his short, beautiful witch. "Tia is an amphibophile," he told us.

"What's that?" Tom asked, taking a step back from her as though she had a rare disease.

"My own term," Sir Thomas said. "An amphibophile is the sort of girl who goes around kissing princes in the hope that one of them will turn into a frog."

Demoiselle Tia smiled up at him, then stood on tiptoe and kissed him on the nose. "Come along," she said to Sylvia. "See your surprise." Hand in hand, the two girls skipped out of sight.

"Hem," Sir Thomas said. "Now to business. I could use your assistance in a brief experiment, if you don't mind."

We assured him that we didn't mind.

"Good. Please come inside." He took us into an inner room where a portly little man was scribbling on a blackboard. "This," he introduced us, "is my good friend Dr. Immanuel Capabella."

The doctor bobbed his head at us, mumbled "A pleasure," and went back to his scribbling.

Sir Thomas took a bunch of papers from a table. "I think we're very close to a complete solution to what's been happening. The only question is whether we'll have enough time. The situation is getting critical. These are the reports of the past few days, and the activity seems to have increased at an alarming rate. There are now so many 'visitors' that the new instructions are to keep them where they arrive unless there is something very special about their story. The last group of them to be sent here arrives today. Here are some of the other reports." He leafed through the papers. "A gigantic building has suddenly appeared on a farm on the East Coast. There are so many people inside of it that the local food supply will have to be augmented. A tribe of natives, who seem to be at war with the Europeans on their own world, have suddenly attacked a town in the Midwest, holding it under siege until guardsmen arrived. Thousands of horseless carriages have appeared on a strip some four miles long and about a hundred feet wide. Also sightings of what you call 'flying saucers' are increasing. One assaulted a group of people at a field where a kite-flying contest was being held. There are hundreds of incidents like this, and the rate is tripling every day. By simple mathematics, the critical point will come inside of two weeks."

"What can we do to help?" I asked.

"We need some final information on what you call the 'blip,' and we're going to get it by a process of congruity. It's the fastest way to check our formulas."

"Fine," Tom agreed. "Onward. You know, you remind me of someone, but I can't figure out who."

"I have a notion about that," Sir Thomas said. "Perhaps some day I'll tell you. Here, please put these rings on." He handed us each a heavy gold ring with an ornate crest and covered with script.

"What now?" I asked, slipping the ring on my finger.

"Now, concentrate. I want you to tell me how close what you are about to experience is to what you call a blip." He took a small piece of paper and wrote a formula, then rolled it up and slid it inside a third ring. *"Alpha,"* he said, waving his stubby wand over the ring and paper, *"et Omega. Simulcron!"*

We were on the other side of the room. Poof, like that. No feeling or anything. One instant we were on one side of the room, and the next we were on the other. "Wow!" I said.

"Was that about it?" Sir Thomas asked.

"That was quite something," Tom said. "I'm impressed."

"Of course. But, was it—did it feel like a blip?"

"No," I told him. "There was no feeling. A blip kind of wrenches your insides."

"Hem. Let's try this." He repeated the process, changing the formula on the paper.

WHAP! We were across the room again, but this time a mule had kicked us en route. "That," I said, checking for broken bones, "was a bit strong. It didn't twist, it slammed."

"Hem. Yes. I think I see what you mean. Let's try again."

The seventh try proved to be the charm. As far as I could tell, it exactly duplicated the feeling of wrenching and dislocating of the blip, and Tom agreed. We did it twice more for luck, and then congratulated each other.

"Michael! Tom! Come see," Sylvia called, running into the room.

"Come see what?" I asked.

"Come on, right outside." She grabbed my arm and pulled me toward the door.

Outside Tia was standing on one foot, looking satisfied, and a white horse was cropping grass beside the path. "Very pretty," I said, looking at the horse.

"Pretty? Is that all you can say?" Sylvia asked. "It's Adolphus!"

Not until then did I notice the twisted, white horn. "Well, well," I said. "So it is. Hello, Adolphus. How've you been?" He lifted his head and stuck out his tongue at me.

"Adolphus!" Sylvia said. "Don't be like that." She put her hands around his neck and petted his mane.

The little man who had been talking to Sir Thomas when we arrived was standing by the side of the path staring at Adolphus. "Say," he said finally, "does he really need all that horn?"

Sylvia stamped her foot. "If you put one hand on him I'll rip off your nose!" she declared.

"I was just asking," the man said, He tipped his white bowler and walked away.

"Don't worry about him," Sir Thomas said. "He won't bother you."

"I'm not worried," Sylvia said. "I warned him."

"Hem."

Sir Thomas told us to go away so he and Dr. Capabella could work, and hoped he'd have something for us that very afternoon.

Then it was time for my surprise.

We went into the main building to go back up to our rooms, after Sylvia promised Adolphus that she'd be down to give him a good brushing as soon as she could find a curry comb. The front hall was crowded with people in a great variety of costumes, obviously the day's group of "visitors."

"Michael!" somebody called. "Theodore Bear!" I turned around to look.

I didn't faint. I admit to turning white and shaking for a minute, but I didn't faint. There, pushing his way through the throng toward me, was Chester.

"Chester?" I croaked.

"What?" Tom said. "I thought you told me . . ."

"Grapgh," I said. "Argh. Chester."

"Hello there," Chester said, slapping me on the shoulder. "I've been looking for you."

"I thought," I said. "I mean, you . . . that is, the last time . . . hello." I looked around for someplace to sit down.

"I must have startled you," Chester said. "I apologize."

"Let's, ah, go upstairs. We can talk there."

"Fine. One second. Dorothy! Oh, Dorothy!" Another figure separated herself from the crowd, and Dorothy joined us. She and Sylvia embraced wordlessly.

"Let's, please, go upstairs," I said. "I don't even want to think about this until I'm sitting down."


"The last thing I know," Chester said, sitting comfortably on the bed with us gathered around him, "is the last thing you know, only the other way around. You and Sylvia were killed—we saw you killed, I won't describe it—and then the last tank went blip. We weren't hurt beyond being shaken up a bit. We blipped a minute later, and found ourselves in the middle of a town. The locals were a suspicious type, they locked us in the hoosegow. We were there for two days, when they decided we were responsible for the disappearance of a little girl. They were coming to lynch us and do other unfriendly things, when we blipped again.

"This time we were in the middle of a deep wood, and spent a day hiding from Indians. Then we blipped again, to this world; and here we are."

"Just think," Tom said. "Somewhere, in some universe, you're both dead. It gives one pause. Wee paws for station identification."

"I guess that's it," I said. "You and I must be from time tracks that lie next to each other; and your Michael and my Chester must actually be dead. Wow."

"The reason I wasn't surprised to see you," Chester said, "is that after I told my story to a Captain LeClerk, he told me that you were here; so I was looking for you. We'll have to compare notes sometime, dredge our memories to see where our worlds differ, if at all. It furthers one to seek the truth."

"They must coincide almost exactly," I said. "Otherwise our history through the blips would be different. Besides, I know the way your memory works. You remember three impossible things before breakfast."

"Yup, that's my Theodore Bear," Chester said. We solemnly shook hands.

# 11

That afternoon Sir Thomas called a meeting, to which we were invited. I introduced Chester to him, and told him what had happened. He hemmed, and nodded. "It had to happen. Perhaps not to you, but it had to happen. It's further proof that you are the perfect people for what we have in mind."

"What's that?" I asked.

"You'll see."

We gathered before a large blackboard and Sir Thomas rolled up his sleeves. "With the assistance of my good friend, Dr. Immanuel Capabella," here the portly little man stood up and took a brief bow, "and the forms of mathematics developed in his world, I—or I should say we—have developed a rather complete theory. We find that it not only explains the, ahem, time-slips sideways that have been taking place, but the prevalence of what we shall call 'magic' on this world and the absence of it on others." He turned to the blackboard. "We have postulated the existence of a new basic particle, which we call the probitron. It does not behave like what we normally think of as a particle. If you prefer, you may consider it a local node in the fabric of the universe. A node that propagates itself at what I am forced to call the 'probable' speed of light, in all directions through the six-dimensional continuum. The basic formula turns out to be extremely simple, which is only right." He wrote:

$$(\text{hex})^2 W = 0$$

"The (hex) squared $W$," he explained, "simply represents the sum of the second partial derivatives of W, the wave function, with respect to the six coordinates of the continuum. Zero, of course, represents nothing. Now, to get an expression for one element of the continuum, we would use:

$$ds^2 = dx^2 + dy^2 + dz^2 - c^2 dt^2 - b^2 du^2 - a^2 dv^2$$

"And further, from the basic laws of magic, we have come up with a third necessary formula, which nicely ties the whole mess together. It may be stated:

$$C = 4Kp^2q^2/r^5$$

"From these, it can easily be seen that," he said, and filled the blackboard with formulas. Dr. Capabella nodded and smiled, while the rest of us stared and looked baffled. At one place Dr. Capabella made a small correction, and Sir Thomas looked pained, but made the erasure.

"Yes," someone called, "but what does all that mean?"

"Wait a minute," Sir Thomas said, going on with his writing. He made a final mark and looked up. "It means that we know what's happening, and what to do about it. At least, what to try."

"What is happening?"

"Someone," Sir Thomas said, "or some group, on some time line, discovered this before we did. Probably way before. For some reason, they don't like us. Before I get to that, let me try to explain how all this works.

"The probitron is the particle of probability. You may think of it as an anti-entropy effect of nature. Out in the, hem, void, where complete randomness and entropy are the rule, there are few probitrons formed. On planets, where there is a mass of matter, a strong gravity field, and more chance for one event causing many other events, the flux of probitrons will be stronger. When the planet develops life, which is the second strongest anti-entropy effect known, the flux is even stronger, and the chance of parallel time track formation increases. Ordinarily a time split, caused by a probitron, will be self-cancelling, and the tracks will close together in, at most, a few microseconds."

"What's the strongest anti-entropy effect?" Chester asked.

"The effect of intelligence. When intelligence develops, even low-order intelligence, parallel time tracks become a fact of the local universe. Their number quickly approaches infinity, as a series of fractions within the unity of the six-dimensional universe. It would be a good way, if we ever explore space, of locating intelligence in any sector. That is, if we can find a way of spotting these fields."

Sir Thomas leaned on the desk and looked serious. "Now, as to what's happening to us. This group, whoever they are, have closed off this, hem, section of time. They've taken a group of parallel time tracks and tied them into a bow. I don't know how large a group, but I'd say it was quite large. Of course, no matter how large it is, since the total number of lines is infinite, the effect is to be thought of as quite localized."

"What does that mean?" someone demanded. "What will that do to us here?"

"It means that the lines aren't parallel any more. They're at acute angles, and getting closer together. In some places they are already, so to speak, rubbing together. That is, the coordinates for places in two lines are becoming congruent, and transfers are happening.

"As my colleague and I see it, what this means is that the lines will finally merge."

"You mean we'll all be thrown together? The whole population of all these worlds will be combined on one? How can we live?"

"I'm afraid it's even worse than that. The probitron flux is different on each world. A high probitron flux here, which means a slight control of probability, is what makes magic possible; even common. In some lines the flux is low enough so that these effects are erratic and uncontrollable. When they come together the fluxes will even out. When the last of them come together, the fluxes will randomize. We will disappear. We will have become improbable."

Lord Gart stood up. "Disappear? Are you sure?"

"I'm afraid so."

"How much time do we have? What can we do?" He looked as if he was ready to run out and mobilize the army.

"I estimate that we have two weeks, and one chance. We are preparing to take that chance."

"What is it?"

Sir Thomas nodded to us. "Please stand up." We did.

"These people," he said, "visitors to our world, are going to become our secret weapon. These five men and women have, in our estimation, the best chance of saving our world—and perhaps the whole human race. I haven't asked them yet; I shall do so now. It will be very dangerous, and I have no way of estimating your chances. I must ask even the ladies, since five is such a small number, but better than three."

"Try leaving us behind," Sylvia stated clearly.

"Then you'll agree to help?"

I tried to think of an appropriate heroic speech.

"Yes," the others said in unison.

"Yes," I agreed lamely.

"Fine. Here's what we have to do. Everyone here was invited for a reason, and will be able to help. First you should know that the latest information confirms our suspicion that our opponents are not human."

A brief babble swept the room and then stopped. Everyone stared at Sir Thomas.

"Our enemies are the inhabitants of what our friends here call the flying saucers. They seem to be survey ships, observing the results of the squeeze. Yesterday one landed a few leagues from here, and some farmers observed the creatures leave the ship. I don't know what they were doing: perhaps effecting repairs, perhaps testing the ground, perhaps eliminating garbage, perhaps eating a picnic lunch; it doesn't matter. Two of the observers are still in shock, but we were able to get a coherent description out of the third. He says they're dragons."

"Dragons?"

"At any rate, they look like dragons. That will do. They are the enemy. Now, here's what we do. First, all military personnel will concentrate on gathering reports on flying saucer activity and interview all 'visitors' on their experiences with the flying saucers. We need all the data we can get. Second, we start an intensive training program on our, hem, assault troops here. We must teach them everything we can about practical magic. Unfortunately, they come from a world where it is in little use."

"Excuse me," someone asked. "But wouldn't it be better, then, to use someone already proficient in the art?"

"We can't. The reason we're using these people is because they have the greatest chance of success. We need people with a high flux of probitrons, people who have gone through as many time changes as possible. These are they."

Lord Gart asked, "Their probability patterns have changed?"

"These five are so improbable," Sir Thomas said, "that if they were to fade away right now and disappear, I wouldn't be at all surprised."

I felt my arm to make sure I was still solid.

"How does that help?" asked Lord Gart.

"In two ways. First, the strong probitron flux will make them highly capable of utilizing the magic we must teach them."

"How long do we have for that?" A man in a peaked wizard's hat asked.

"I estimate that our margin of safety leaves four days."

"Four days! Why, it takes fifteen years to achieve any sort of competence."

"I know. It's quite a challenge, isn't it? Luckily we can concentrate in certain fields. Secondly, it makes it much more likely that they'll be able to get picked up."

Something went cold inside of me. "Picked up?"

"Yes, of course. By a flying saucer. That's the whole point."

"Oh," I said.

The four days went fast. I don't remember much except getting yelled at a lot and not sleeping. When it was over, we had learned certain spells and methods that would be of most use to us. How to disappear. How to blip from one place to another (excuse the word blip). How to create and use a simulacrum, if we got the chance. Things like that. Sylvia turned out to be the most apt pupil, Tom next, Dorothy next, then Chester and me. Chester, during the final day of instruction, had occasion to refer to the *I Ching,* and his instructor got excited and called in Sir Thomas.

"Do you know how to use that book?" Sir Thomas asked.

"I've been using it for years," Chester said, insulted.

"Well, remember, now, it has much stronger powers than you're used to. It may come in handy."

Then we got a good, solid four hours sleep, and it was time for our final indoctrination.

"We've done the best we can," Sir Thomas said. "Now it's up to you. We've plotted the appearances of the flying saucers, and found a pattern. We can take you to the area one will most certainly appear in. You have to get aboard, but don't worry about it. With your pattern, it's almost inevitable that they'll take you. To this small extent, their weapon will work against them."

"What then?" I asked.

"Use your eyes and other senses that come in handy. You must find and destroy the machine that's doing this. It has to be a machine of some sort, and it has to be located right in the center of the closing time lines, which is where their base must be. That's all I can tell you."

"If we succeed in this," Sylvia asked, "what will happen to us?"

"Everyone who is displaced along the continuum should return to their own world. This will happen within two minutes of the time you destroy the machine, and it will happen all at once, with a snap. If it happens at all. If the process has gone too far, if the lines are permanently warped, nothing will happen. The process will continue to its inevitable end. Good luck."

"That means we'll separate," Sylvia said, holding my hand.

"Well, hem, if you wish to remain together, try holding hands tightly when the snap comes. That may equalize the fluxes and send you all to the home line of whichever of you has the least probitron pattern. I promise nothing, but it may work. If it doesn't, with the information I have now I should work out a method of traveling between the lines fairly soon. A few years at most. I'll come to visit all of you." He shook hands with each of us in turn. "I repeat, good luck. I wish we could have done more."

# 12

Sylvia said a long good-bye to her unicorn, and promised it that it would be home soon. I could have sworn I saw a tear in the corner of the beast's eye as we walked away. We were taken by coach to a nearby town and instructed to go up to the roof of the town hall. There we waited. Below us, the town went through its usual market-day activities, the only abnormality being the large number of people in unusual clothing. This was one of the towns where the visitors were being billeted.

Sylvia pointed to the sky. "Look!"

A saucer was descending straight down over the town square. A few seconds later the townspeople saw it, and went shrieking off in all directions. The saucer darted down, and thick purple beams flashed out, drawing people and any loose objects they hit into the ship.

"The thing doesn't see us!" Sylvia shouted. "Gome here, thing!" She picked up a couple of loose roofing tiles and hurled them at the saucer. They fell far short, and it kept ignoring us. In a few minutes it stopped collecting, as the square was empty, and rose ponderously into the air, heading away from us.

"This is unfair!" Sylvia said.

Dorothy got up and waved. "Come here, little saucer." A second later we were all up and waving like lunatics.

The saucer paused for a moment, seeming to make up its mind, then it flashed toward us, darting out a purple beam.

We were in a whirlwind. We were motionless in free fall, surrounded by black. Then we were in a large bin, surrounded by people. It was as quick as that.

Most of the people were yelling or screaming hysterically, or kicking and clawing at the walls; we were an island of calm in the midst of the storm.

"Well," Chester said, "step one."

"What now?" I asked.

"Now we wait until we get where we're going."

The saucer made several more stops on the way. We could tell because every now and then new people would appear in the bin, until finally there was hardly enough room to sit down. Aside from that there was no sensation of motion.

We were yanked out of the bin by the same method we had been put in, and found ourselves in a large hall of some sort. It could have been an underground cavern, or merely a gigantic building, we had no way of telling. We were on polished concrete that stretched off in all directions. Above us, suspended from the high ceiling, were metal catwalks like the ones used in prisons. Scattered throughout the giant room were circular, waist-high cubicles that I found out contained toilet facilities.

"Humph," I said, sitting down next to where Chester was squatting on the floor. "Again, oh leader, what now?"

"Again we wait," Chester said. "They must have brought us here for something."

"Yes," Tom said. "Probably for food."

"Tom!" Dorothy said, looking shocked. "Surely they're not cannibals."

"How do you know? Besides, for a dragon to eat a human is not cannibalism."

"If you can't think of something cheerful," Sylvia instructed him, "don't think at all."

There was a clanking sound above us, and I looked up. One of the dragons was approaching on the catwalk. As it got closer, I could see what it was. A ten-foot dinosaur, wearing a bright red belt. It passed by us humming a high-pitched note monotonously.

"That's funny," Dorothy said, staring at the creature as it went by.

"Hilarious," I agreed.

"What's funny, Dorothy?" Sylvia asked.

"I could hear it."

"So could I," Chester said. "Most unmusical."

"That's not what I meant I could sort of hear inside its head. I know what it was thinking."

Chester stood up. "What? Really?"

"Unless I was imagining it."

"We'll assume you weren't. What was it thinking?"

"Something like, 'Well, I've done that batch, Now all I have to do is feed the greks and I can relax for a while.'"

"Greks?"

"Yes. The impression was that he meant us."

"Maybe," I suggested, "this is a sort of gigantic petshop, and greks are their favorite pets."

"Could be," Tom agreed. "And then again, maybe greks are to them what skeet are to us."

"Skeet?" Sylvia asked.

There was a gurgling sound from somewhere above us, and it rained blue grapefruit. Some of them bounced when they hit, the rest just flattened out and lay there.

"That must be grek food," Chester said, picking up a flattened grapefruit and examining it.

"We're being assaulted by dinner," I said.

Sylvia grabbed one of the bouncing ones as it went by. "I wonder what it does?" she said.

"Let's see." I took it and looked it over. "It seems to be some sort of soft plastic. It's perfectly round. No, it's not; there's a bump on it" I pressed the bump in, and was rewarded by a stream of water in my face.

"Ah!" Tom said. "It's a portable drinking fountain. Think it's safe?"

"Sure." I wiped my face. "Why should they bother trying to poison us?"

"This one's food," Chester said. He displayed the one he was holding, which had split open like an overripe sausage. Inside was a brown, glutinous mess resembling sticky bread pudding.

"You know," I said, "if they're feeding us, they must be planning to keep us here for some time. We can't do anything from here."

"Right," Chester agreed. "First job is to get out. Fine. How?"

Tom rested his chin on his fist "Aye," he agreed, "there's the rub."

"Do you think the magic we learned will work here?" Dorothy asked.

"It should," Tom told her. "If this is the center of the disturbance, as Sir Thomas assumed, then the probitron flux here should be even higher than on his world."

"Let's try it then," Dorothy said. She took a deep breath, closed her eyes, drew a symbol in the air, and disappeared.

"Dorothy?" I called.

"Like that," she yelled from behind me. I turned around. She was walking back toward us, threading her way among a group of surprised-looking Confederate soldiers.

"Great," Chester said, when she had returned. "What do we do, keep flipping from side to side in the hall until one of the monsters comes to find out what's happening?"

"No," Dorothy said. "Just one flip." She pointed to the catwalk. "Up there."

"Say," Tom said. "It's an idea."

"I don't know," I said. "We've only jumped on one plane. Sir Thomas said something about not using it to go up or down because of the law of conservation of energy."

Sylvia put her hand on my shoulder. "Michael," she said patiently, as if explaining to a small boy, "it's only about fifteen feet. And it's only this once. We can break a law once, in a good cause, can't we?"

"It's not that sort of law," I said, "but never mind. I guess we have to do something, and this looks like the best bet."

"Okay," Chester said. "I think we'd all better stick together, so let's go."

"Now?" I said. "I mean, shouldn't we drink some water first, or something? Do some deep breathing? Maybe sleep for a while?"

"No," Chester said. "Now."

"Right. I was just asking."

"We'd better go separately," Chester said. "You first."

"Me?" I asked. "First? Right. Just what I was going to suggest myself."

I examined a small area of the catwalk carefully, fixing it in my mind, then closed my eyes, made the protective sign that was mine alone, and muttered the invocation.

My knees buckled. I felt like I had just landed after falling too far. With a great effort of will, and by putting both hands out in front of me, I managed not to go flat on my face.

I was on the catwalk; bruised but undaunted.

One by one my comrades in arms appeared around me—falling. Everyone fell forward except Chester, who sat heavily and turned red.

"Woof!" Sylvia said. "What was that?"

"That," I told her, "was the universe exacting instant retribution for the law we just broke."

"Oh," she said. "You meant *that* kind of law."

"What now, boss?" I asked.

"I think we should now consult a higher oracle," Chester said.

"You mean . . ."

"Yes. The *Ching.*" He took out his three coins and made the first cast.

"Now?" I asked. "What if somebody—or something—comes along?"

Chester said, "Don't let them disturb me until I'm finished."

We sat there on this catwalk, fifteen feet above the ground, until Chester finished casting the coins.

"Well?" I asked. "What does your ancient Chinese friend have to say?"

"It says Grace, changing to Coming to Meet." He took out his portable reader. "The changes are interesting. Hmm. Grace tells us that it is favorable to undertake something."

"That's good," Tom said. "What?"

"It doesn't say. However, the changes tell us to lend grace to our toes and to the beard on our chin. Also to come as if on wings. Humiliation, but in the end, good fortune."

"What does all that mean?" I asked.

"Any ideas?" Chester asked. "After all, this is supposed to be a community project."

"Lending grace to our toes," Dorothy suggested, "is probably telling us to get out of here fast. But I don't know about the beard on my chin."

Tom snapped his fingers. "I've got it! Of course. Beards are the classical symbols of a disguise."

"What sort of disguise do you suggest?" I asked. "Postmen?"

"Why not look like the dragons themselves?" Sylvia asked.

"They're not dragons," I told her. "They're dinosaurs."

"How do we manage to look like them?" Chester asked.

"I can do a shape-change spell. Can't you?"

"Right!" Tom said. "I guess I'm not used to this magic yet."

"Wait a minute," I said. "I think I could manage a dog, but I don't know about a dinosaur."

"All right," Chester said. "We'll put you on a leash and bring you along."

We practiced, up there suspended fifteen feet above our fellow greks, until we could approximate dinosaurs fairly well. I have no idea what the people below thought was happening, if any of them noticed. When we had the dinosaur bit down pat, we flipped a coin and went in the *heads* direction along the catwalk.

"Stick together," Chestersaur directed. "If we run into any of these beasts, just keep walking."

"With an air of such ineffable dignity," Tom added, "that no one who sees us could doubt that we were on official business."

"Very good," I said. "Tell me, what does a dinosaur do to look dignified?" It felt funny, talking with a dinosaur's mouth. Of course this was just a form of projection, not true shape-changing, but still, even to *me* I looked like a dinosaur.

We reached the end of the catwalk and entered a maze of corridors and rooms. There were no doors or partitions of any kind, and all the rooms seemed to be empty. Completely empty—no dinosaurs, no furniture, no rugs, drapes, pictures or anything: just floors and walls. Off ahead of us, a dinosaur flitted out of a room to the left and disappeared into a room on the right.

We went further into the maze, picking our directions at random. An occasional dinosaur hurried by, intent on some mission of its own and hardly giving us a glance. We all froze when the first one passed, but gained confidence when we were ignored.

"They don't believe in furniture," Tom commented.

"What would you do with furniture if you were a dinosaur?" Chester asked.

A tall dinosaur turned the corner and jabbed a claw at us. *"Crackle, groar, rang ring grek grak gibble fapfop!"* it said. Then, with a high, keening whistle, it raced off down the hall.

"What was all that about?" I wondered.

Dorothy said, "We're all to assemble on the main chamber. In seven *gibbles* the warp will be permanent, and we will have achieved the final solution to the grek problem. It is to roar."

"That's what he said?" Chester asked.

"That's what he was thinking while he spoke," she assured us.

"How long is a gibble?" I asked.

Dorothy shrugged her large, green shoulders. "How should I know?"

"Let's hope it's hours and not seconds," Chester said. "I wonder where the main chamber is."

"Down around that way, to the left," Dorothy told him.

"Well! What else did you pick up?"

Dorothy blushed. "Nothing," she said. We didn't push.

Around to the left, no more than five or six blocks away, we came to the main chamber. Furniture or no furniture, these creatures built big rooms. This one was about three times the size of the largest train station I've ever been in: just one bare room, no decoration, no pillars. It was crawling with green dinosaurs.

In the center of this vast hall was a three-story cast iron nightmare. A combination of boiler pipes and angle irons, it twisted around and took turns that the eye couldn't follow.

I nudged Chester. "Think that's it?" I asked.

"It had better be," he said.

"How," Tom asked, "do we take it?"

"Let's look it over," Dorothy suggested.

We approached the machine, just five more dinosaurs in the crowd. One side of it had a series of meters, clicking off geometric shapes at varying rates. The far side had a nozzle about three feet off the floor, behind a waist-high (if I had a waist) stone barrier. From the nozzle, a beam of blue haze projected out to hit a large, carefully machined dull-colored block about forty feet away. The beam then split into waves, which flowed over the block and faded out.

"That's it!" Chester declared.

"What now?" I asked.

"Now we deflect that beam."

"With what?" I asked.

"With ourselves," Chester told me.

"How's that again?"

"Sure. That's a probitron beam. Actually, what you're seeing probably isn't the beam, but ionized air surrounding the beam. We are carrying a high probitron charge. Like charges repel; therefore we would repel the beam. Simple."

"The thought repels me," I told him. "But what the hell, you only live however many times you live."

We advanced toward the beam. As we got closer I felt something tugging at me, like being in a wind that permeated my whole body. Chester, in front of me, looked annoyed. He raised a hand. A hand?

"*Grek!*" something yelled. "*Brekabrek grek!*" The nearest dinosaur jumped away from us like a horse from a rattlesnake.

We had lost our disguise. The probitron wind had ripped our magical covering right off.

While other dinosaurs got out of the way, several large ones with red belts were converging around us.

"Move it!" I yelled. We raced toward the stone wall.

A large claw grabbed at me, and I twisted around and pulled away, leaving part of my shirt behind.

A large dinosaur clutched Dorothy, lifting her in the air like a lobster, while she kicked and yelled.

A squad of beasts formed between us and the beam. Sylvia leaped up on my shoulders and launched herself through the air, over their line.

She was intercepted, and brought down.

The line headed toward me.

Chester, while the attention was focused on the aerial display, dived between a pair of dinosaur legs and reached the wall. He swung himself over.

*"Maggagak grek!"* a dinosaur yelled, and the line turned and dove for Chester.

He fell backward, into the beam.

Time stopped. Everything froze but Chester and the beam. It bounced off him, scattering around the room.

Then he had disappeared, and the beam was back.

He reappeared, and the beam deflected.

Disappeared.

Back.

Gone.

Back.

Chester flickered in and out of existence about every quarter second, and time, where we were, came back to normal. The dinosaurs stared at Chester, but made no move to grab him.

The room started to rumble, softly, in a quarter-second rhythm.

The machine started to visibly shake.

There was a cracking sound, and the beam disappeared. Pieces of machine clattered to the floor.

The first piece of ceiling fell. Then the next.

The dinosaurs honked wildly and headed for the exits.

Within a minute, we were alone in the hall. The ceiling kept falling.

I raced over to the wall and pulled Chester, who was barely conscious, over to my side, to get him out of the way of falling parts.

"Michael! Chester!" Sylvia yelled. "Come here fast. Hold hands. Michael, I love you."

# BLIP

# 13

We were back in our own time line, Chester, Tom and I. Sylvia, Dorothy and, I presume, Adolphus, are back with the circus.

Sir Thomas, if you read this, I can be reached through my agent, Seligmann & Collier.

# APPENDIX

For those interested in the math of probitron theory and parallel time tracks, I have reconstructed what I can remember of the equations of Doctor Capabella. My thanks for the aid of Michael Anderson in this project. Any obvious stupid mistakes are, of course, my own.

As an extension of Minkowski 4-space, the spatial coordinates,

$$x = x_1$$

$$y = x_2$$

$$z = x_3$$

and temporal coordinates,

$$ict = x_4$$

are now extended with the pseudo-temporal coordinates,

$$jbu = x_5$$

$$kav = x_6$$

forming a six-dimensional continuum.

[Note that $i, j, k$ are Hamilton's Quarterain operators, which have the properties:

$$i^2 = j^2 = k^2 = -1$$

and:

$$ij = -ji = k,$$

$$jk = -kj = i,$$

$$ki = -ik = j\,]$$

The Capabellan equation:

$$(\text{hex})^2 y = 0$$

where $(\text{hex})^2$ is the Capabellan Operator,

$$(\text{hex})^2 = \nabla^2 = \frac{1}{c^2}\frac{\partial^2}{\partial t^2} - \frac{1}{b^2}\frac{\partial^2}{\partial u^2} - \frac{1}{a^2}\frac{\partial^2}{\partial v^2}$$

that is to say:

$$\frac{\partial^2 y}{\partial x^2} + \frac{\partial^2 y}{\partial y^2} + \frac{\partial^2 y}{\partial z^2} - \frac{1}{c^2}\frac{\partial^2 y}{\partial t^2} - \frac{1}{b^2}\frac{\partial^2 y}{\partial u^2} - \frac{1}{a^2}\frac{\partial^2 y}{\partial v^2} = 0$$

where $c$ is the speed of light, and $b$ & $a$ are the first and second probitronic propagation pseudo-velocities.

The contact potential function in the six-space continuum is:

$$U(r) = \frac{E^4}{r^4}$$ where $r$ is the distance from the contactual charge, $E$.

The Contact Intensity Vector in three-space:

$$\vec{c} = -4\vec{r}\,\frac{E^4}{r^6}$$

where $\overset{\shortmid}{r}$ is the distance vector.

Contactual flux in three-space:

$$\mathbf{f}_c = -8\mathbf{p}\,\frac{E^4}{r^3}$$

The three-space Harmonic equation for a contactual field is:

$$\nabla^2 u = -8\mathbf{p}\,\frac{E^4}{r^3}$$

where $\nabla^2$ is the Laplacian operator so that:

$$\nabla^2 u = \frac{\partial^2 u}{\partial x^2} + \frac{\partial^2 u}{\partial y^2} + \frac{\partial^2 u}{\partial z^2} = 8\mathbf{p}\,\frac{E^4}{r^3}$$

Some known criteria for Merger of Universe$_1$ & Universe$_2$.

$$\hat{\imath} > \frac{|E_2 - E_1|}{V}$$

II) The Probitronic "Inertial" relationships:

$$\mathbf{z} > \frac{|L_2 - L_1|}{V} \qquad \mathbf{g} > \frac{|N_2 - N_1|}{V}$$

III) The Entropy Relationship:

$$\Sigma > \frac{|H_2 - H_1|}{V}$$

Where $V = V_t = V_1 = V_2$ is the volumns of the two universes that will merge. The volumns must be equal. And where $\in$, $\zeta$, $\Upsilon$, $\Sigma$ are constants.

# AUTHOR'S BIOGRAPHY

Mister Kurland is a thin, tense young man with wire-rimmed glasses and the perpetually frightened look of a rabbit with an invitation to lunch at the Lion's Club. He has a Doctorate in Ecdysiology, and his first published work was his thesis: *Cultural Patterns of Migrant Brooklyn Apple-Pickers With Reference to the Prevalence, Utility, Adaptability and Social Standing of Ecdysiasts Within the Group-Standard Milieu.* It was published as an illustrated children's book under the title *She Stripped for Cider,* and went into three printings.

He has worked as a wire-stapler, a barrel-staver, a window-washer, a herring-kipperer, a Scotch-tippler and a peck-of-pickled-peppers-picker. This diversified background has given him the wealth of experience which has so far proved totally useless for writing science fiction.

He is now living and working on a houseboat on the Dhama river in Northern Thibeth, but will soon be moving back to the United States as he finds it hard to concentrate during the six hours a day in which the boat is submerged. His present project is a dictionary which will conform to his unique ideas regarding English spelling.